ACTS OF
Grace

A MEN OF WRATH NOVEL

ACTS OF Grace

A MEN OF WRATH NOVEL

ELEANOR ALDRICK

Acts of Grace
Copyright © 2021 by Eleanor Aldrick

Cover Design: Sinfully Seductive Designs
Interior Formatting: Sinfully Seductive Designs

This is a work of fiction. Names, characters, businesses, places, events, locales, and incidents are either the products of the author's imagination or used in a fictitious manner. Any resemblance to actual persons, living or dead, or actual events is purely coincidental.

FIRST EDITION
ISBN: 978-1-7345272-5-4
10 9 8 7 6 5 4 3 2 1

For the dreamers.

Chase after your visions with abandon, for there is only one life to live.

Grit for when they are too blind to see,
Grace for when their veil has been lifted.

—Eleanor Aldrick

Playlist
ON REPEAT

HALSEY: YOU SHOULD BE SAD

AVICI: WAKE ME

TIESTO: THE BUSINESS

SHAWN MENDES, JUSTIN BIEBER:
MONSTER

NINE INCH NAILS: THE DAY THE
WORLD WENT AWAY

FUTURE: LIFE IS GOOD

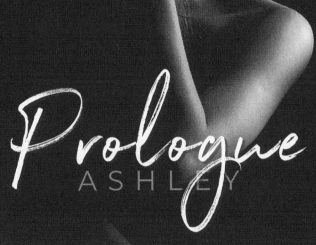

Prologue
ASHLEY

His car isn't here.

His *fucking* car. Isn't. Here.

I scan the text message one more time. Maybe, just maybe, I read it wrong.

That's possible, right? This could all be...

Nope.

Sure as fuck, the text reads loud and clear.

SORRY BABE. I'm not feeling too good. I'm going to call it early and crash. Hope it's just a 24hr bug. -xoxo

My chest tightens as I look at his open garage, devoid of his silver BMW. The only vehicle visible is his little brother's Harley.

My hands shake and my throat goes dry as I grab my bag and

the chicken noodle soup I'd picked up on the way here.

Maybe there's a logical explanation for everything. Maybe his brother took his car out. *The very car he lets no one drive…*

Placing one foot in front of the other, I slowly make my way to the front door as my head plays a volley of excuses on loop.

Unable to put off the inevitable, I lift my hand and knock, praying against all odds that my gut instinct is wrong.

One Mississippi, two Mississippi, three–

"Ashley? What are you doing here? Brad isn't home."

The small fissure in my chest spreads into a full-blown valley of sorrow, and the ache in my heart threatens to swallow me whole.

Thanks to southern manners and quick thinking, I'm able to recover without his brother noticing.

"Oh, I know. I told him I was bringing him something and he asked me to bring it by and wait for him." Putting on my most convincing smile, I walk in as if I own the place. "I'll just wait in his room. I don't want to keep you from your night."

The twenty-year-old simply shrugs as a female voice calls from his bedroom, beckoning for him to return. "Whatever. You know where the fridge is."

"Sure do. Night, Jacob."

"Night."

I beeline it straight to the liar's room. I want to surprise my dear boyfriend, after all.

Placing the container of soup on the dresser, I check the clock.

Nine Thirty.

Blowing out a nervous breath, I question whether what I'm doing is sane. Am I blowing things out of proportion, inventing things in my head?

The gnawing in the pit of my stomach tells me I'm not.

Coming to terms with reality, I lower myself onto the bed, my entire body vibrating with anxious nerves while I do.

Looking at my phone, I sit here and wait.

And wait.

And wait.

And wait.

It isn't until one thirty in the morning that I hear the front door open and shut, followed by the unmistakable giggle of a female and the loud shushing I know all too well.

Not a minute later, the bedroom door swings open and a sloppy drunken tangle of limbs comes barreling through.

Amazingly enough, Brad and his side chick continue to make out, oblivious to the fact that I'm in the room.

Looking at the woman closely, I see it's his freaking secretary. Rage floods through me, causing the beat of my heart to thud loudly in my ears.

How long has this been going on? How long have I been played the fool?

I sit there gawking at the man I've dedicated my life to for the past year.

College is supposed to be fun, but instead of enjoying my last year at Howard, I spent it at boring client dinners or stupid galas—all to please the man standing before me, shoving his tongue down this redhead's throat.

"If I wanted a cheating high-society asshole, I could've stayed in Dallas," I mumble under my breath.

Having enough of the show being portrayed before me, I jump into action.

With shaky legs, I stand, making my way to the container of soup before opening it.

Before my mind can register what I'm doing, the entire contents of the now tepid soup are being hurled at the two people in front of me.

"What the—?!"

"Aaagh!"

A slow smile spreads across my lips as my chest vibrates with rage, "Right. Well, I see you're feeling better." Grabbing my purse, I move to exit but not before issuing my replacement a warning, "I'd make him go down on you first. He never lasts more than a minute once inside."

ACTS OF GRACE

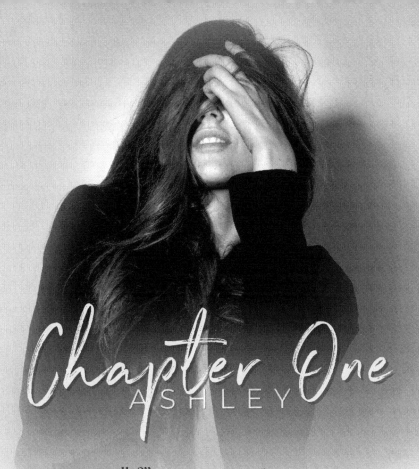

Chapter One
ASHLEY

"Hello?"

A rich male voice comes through the line and my body stills. Of all the people who could've picked up, it had to be him.

"Hey, Titus." I suck in a ragged breath and try to compose myself. The last thing I want is to divulge my humiliating situation to my brother's best friend. "Can you please put William on the line?"

"What's the matter, kid?" His gravelly voice is demanding. Much like the man behind the phone.

"I need him to send the jet. I want to come home." My voice cracks on the last word. Dallas hasn't been home for years, but the idea of remaining in this place one moment longer has me wanting to crawl out of my own skin.

"Head to the hanger." His words tinged with anger are the last thing I hear before the line goes dead.

My breath stutters and my chest tightens as I fight the urge to shed another tear.

Titus isn't one to share emotions and the idea of him comforting anyone is laughable, so I'm not sure why his abrupt dismissal cuts me even deeper.

What was I expecting? A full-on gab session with my bestie?

Shaking my head, I pull back onto the highway and head to the familiar hangar. In a couple of hours I'll be back in Texas. A place with its own set of dark memories. Memories that will forever haunt me.

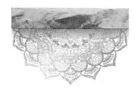

Titus

My grip tightens around the rocks glass as I stare out into the darkness of the night sky. A two-hour flight has felt like a ten-hour trip across the world. I'd give anything to make time move faster.

What the fuck has her so worked up? Whatever or whoever did this to her will pay. I'll make sure of it.

The last time I heard her this upset was three years ago. I'll never forget the call that changed our worlds forever.

"Titus, thank fuck you picked up. I've been trying to reach the whole crew." William, one of my best friends, *is panic stricken. The anguish tangible through the receiver.*

"I'm here, brother. What's up?"

"Ashley." He chokes on his sister's name and my body goes rigid.

Ashley. The lanky girl turned awkward teenager and now forbidden fruit. *"William. Talk to me. Is your sister okay?"*

"My dad. I need you to..." he sobs into the phone and my lunch threatens to come up. Shit must be bad if he's crying. I've never once seen this man shed a tear, let alone sob.

"Tell me. What do you need?"

"Please. Go to the house and get Ashley out." He sniffs, sucking in a breath before continuing. *"The cops are on their way, but I want one of us there with her. She's been sheltered her whole life. Damn it, man."*

"I'm on my way." I don't bother asking what happened. Whatever it is, I'll be there. Though we aren't blood, we're still family and I'll never let my brothers down.

"Thank you, Titus. I have to warn you. It's bad. Ashley called me in hysterics, and it took me a good fifteen minutes to get her to say something that made sense. Fuck. I never got along with the old man but, damn, I didn't want him to go out like this."

"Are you coming home soon?"

"Yes. I'm messaging my professors and am heading out on the first flight home. I just wish it were me who'd walked in on Dad. Not poor Ashley."

"Walked in?" My face contorts as I picture what Ashley could've seen.

"Yeah, man. It's bad. I have no clue what sick fuck did this to him, to our family. But mark my words, there isn't a corner on this earth where they'll be able to hide."

I pull up to the massive estate smack dab in the middle of Highland Park, one of the most prestigious neighborhoods in all of Texas, and the first thing I see is Ashley's G-Wagon in that horrible shade of powder pink.

"I'm here but I don't see your sister, just her car."

"Fuck. She must still be inside. You need to get her out of there and keep her safe until I get back."

"Ten-four. I'll call you once we're back at my place."

I cut the line and shove my phone into my pocket.

If I thought William's words had prepared me for what I was about to walk into, man was I wrong.

Blood. Crimson blood smeared from the foyer straight into the hall and along the walls.

I pick up the pace as I follow the trail of death into the study where I see a grief-stricken face huddled in the corner, rolled into herself like a frightened child. She doesn't even acknowledge that someone has entered the room, her swollen red eyes are focused behind the desk.

Following her line of vision, I see something I'll never be able to unsee.

Her father's decapitated body lying in a pool of his own blood. And if that weren't disturbing enough, all of his appendages have been removed.

"POLICE," a voice booms from the hall.

"In here!" I shout, heading toward Ashley's huddled

frame. Picking her up off the floor, I press her into my chest and whisper into her hair, "Shhh, kid. I've got you."

Walking toward the hallway, I'm met with two officers, guns drawn. "About time you showed up. If you don't mind, I'm removing the victim's daughter from the scene. If you need her, we'll be at the front of the home."

The head officer narrows his eyes, but I can't give two fucks. They should've been the first to arrive and the fact that I was here before they were, should be grounds for their termination. I know Dallas isn't small and this neighborhood rarely sees this type of crime, but damn, that's no excuse.

"Titus, I presume. William called and informed us you'd be here. Please don't leave the grounds. We'll have questions for you and Ms. Hawthorne."

"No problem." I walk past them, not wanting to spend a moment longer inside these stifling walls.

"Titus?" Ashley's big brown eyes look up at me, her face scrunched up and panicked.

"Shhh. I've got you, Min skatt. Always have. Always will."

A gust of air hits me in the face, signaling the opening of the cabin door and breaking me from my memories. Looking up from my glass I see a pair of long legs grace me with their presence, followed by what could only be described as the most beautiful woman to ever walk this earth.

Ashley was always a beautiful child, but when she blossomed into a woman, there was no denying what she was—*fucking gorgeous.*

21

We constantly had to play defense, letting all the high school boys know William's kid sister was off limits, including to our inner circle.

Ashley brushes long brown waves off of her tear-stricken face and my heart squeezes. The thought of someone hurting her makes me see red. My fists clench and my jaw tightens, "Who *fucking* did this to you?"

"Well, hello to you too." Ashley attempts to feign a smile, but I see through it. I see right through her.

"Who. Did. This." Each word coming out staccato, not a question, but a demand.

Unfortunately for me, it was apparently the wrong move. Ashley bursts into hysterical sobbing, pushing me to act without thinking.

Getting up from my seat, I wave away the stewardess and signal her for takeoff. As soon as I reach Ashley, I scoop her into my arms and carry her to the bedroom at the back of the jet.

This isn't a scene I want anyone else to witness, and I know she'd appreciate the privacy.

As we reach the door, her body violently shakes against mine, her tears soaking through my shirt and making the material stick to my chest. *Shit. Fuck. Shit.* I don't deal with emotions well and this situation is going from bad to worse.

"I. Just. Caaaaan't," Ashley bellows into my chest, "Stop. Cryyyying." Her big eyes look up at mine, pleading, supplicating, demanding help.

Doing the only thing I can think of, I shut the door behind me and press her back against the door. If she wants help, I'll give it to her. Even if it's the only way I know how.

Unbuckling my belt, I yank it off, taking her delicate little wrists and placing them above her head. Looking down at her, I tie the belt around her arms and loop them over the coat hook on the door.

Damn, how fucked up is this? Should I stop? Fuck, this is William's little sister!

"Ashley, tell me if you want me to stop."

Biting her trembling lip, she looks up at me through her wet lashes, but shakes her head.

"Ashley, use your words. I won't do this if you don't want me to."

Sniffling, her mouth goes slack before her tongue darts out to lick her bottom lip, her hungry eyes full of lust lock on to mine before she answers. "Don't stop."

Well, damn. With her looking at me like that, there's not a man in this world that could stop me.

Not even William.

Chapter Two
ASHLEY

My lip quivers as I take in the sight before me. The untouchable man of my dreams stands, jaw clenched and brows furrowed. The inner battle waging behind those baby blues almost makes me feel guilty for wanting what I want. *Almost.*

God. I must be ten shades of fucked up for wanting him to take me right after the ordeal I went through, but all I feel is hunger. All I want is mind numbing bliss.

"Please don't make me beg." My wet lashes bat against my hot flesh, a full-bodied flush enveloping me and threatening to eat me whole.

"*Min skatt*, if we do this, there's no going back. Do you understand?"

His childhood name for me sends shivers down my back in the most delicious way, and I'm left feeling all sorts of knotted up inside. I know I want him, and I know it's not smart to jump into bed with someone right after a breakup, but I can't bring myself to care. All I can do is throw caution to the wind for this man.

He's been the forbidden friend I could never have. The man I lusted over, sure he'd never see me the way I saw him. But now? Now he sees me, and fuck if I won't take full advantage of that.

Ex-boyfriend? What ex-boyfriend?

Lifting a leg up and around him, I try to bring him toward me. With our eyes locked, I nod. "I understand. I don't want to go back."

Titus runs a hand across his face, forming a fist at his lips and biting it with a groan. "Ashley Hawthorne, you'll be the death of me. But fuck if it won't be worth the ride."

Reaching up, his hands trail down my arms and follow the curve of my body—over my breasts, down the dip of my waist and squeezing in an almost painful grip. "Wha—"

A hand reaches up, his calloused thumb rubbing across my lips, "Shhh. Let me take care of you the only way I know how. If you want me to stop, all you have to do is say the word diamond."

My brows push together, but I can't help but smile. I'm not sure why the idea of this serious man picking a word like diamond makes my lips curl upward.

"Tell me you understand, little treasure, or this stops here."

My eyes narrow and my smile turns into a snarl, "Don't you dare leave me like this."

"There's that fire I love so much." A wicked grin spreads across his gorgeous mouth as my stomach flutters at the use of the word love.

Get it together, girl. Do *not* put words in his mouth. That's probably what got me in trouble with—"Agh."

Titus rips off my skirt with one hard pull, the fabric tugging at my hips. "Remember, diamond."

"Mhm." I nod, eagerly awaiting his next move.

I don't know what I was expecting, but it definitely wasn't *this*.

Titus lowers onto his knees, gripping the backside of my thighs and lifting them on to his shoulders, placing my aching core right in front of his delectable mouth. His eyes meet mine as his tongue reaches out, licking my slit through the already dampened lace.

My body shudders at the sensation of the fabric and wetness rubbing against my sensitive nub. "Don't tease me, please."

I feel Titus smile against my lips before his teeth nip at the delicate fabric, pulling it up and against me, creating even more torturous friction. His gorgeous smile grows wider as I whimper in a combination of need and frustration.

Releasing my panties from his mouth, he licks his lips. "Remember, use your word if you want me to stop."

"Oh, I see what you're doing. Well, two can play at that game. Just you wait until it's my turn." I pout, trying to bite back the grin that so desperately wants to escape.

In that moment, a multitude of emotions flash through his eyes and I can't quite figure them all out. Was that sadness I saw?

Before I can ask, he's back at lavishing my body with his mouth.

His teeth place gentle nips on my inner thigh as he works his way up from the inside of my knee to right where I need him the most. Right when I think he's about to give me what I want, he repeats the entire process on the other thigh.

Refusing to play this game any longer, I take the bottom of my feet and press them against his back, pulling him and his face toward me. "Please Titus, I need you."

With another quick tug, the black lace covering me is ripped away, the coolness of the air adding to the heightened sensations driving me mad. "Let's get one thing straight. I gave you your word for a reason. I'm not gentle and I don't play nice. You'll come hard, but only when I say so."

Before I can protest, his lips have latched on to me, his tongue undulating and coaxing my hips to buck with every pull of his mouth.

God, if this is him not playing nice, I'll take asshole Titus every single damn day. "Mmmm, more."

Titus growls into me as his hands grab on to my ass and squeeze, his fingers digging into the plump flesh with such force that I'll be sure to have little reminders long after this tryst is over.

Not wanting to fade into the sadness of his loss, I dive back into the moment, bucking myself into him every time he threatens with the retreat of his tongue.

"Fuck. You taste so damn good, baby." Titus' lips vibrate over my needy pussy, wanting him to keep going.

"Words, later. Sucking and licking, now. Agh!" I arch my back as he inserts three fingers into me, stretching me and making me need more.

"That's what you get, little brat." He applies pressure to a spot I never knew existed, making my entire body shake and my vision begin to darken. "*Min skatt*, you belong to me. Every part of you is mine and I won't stop until I've owned every inch of your body."

His words fade in and out as the world around me goes black.

What the fuck is this magic?!

My legs violently quiver against his stubble as he continues his assault. His thick fingers pumping in and out, heating my body and making it catch fire as his mouth relentlessly sucks my clit.

"My god, Titus."

"Yes, baby." I feel him grin against my core before one of his fingers circles the tight ring of muscles near my entrance. "You can call me god now… but wait until I've wrecked every inch of you."

I moan deliriously as he plays my body like a violin. "I'll call you whatever you want. Just. Don't. Stop."

Titus lets out a feral growl, his hands slipping out of me and trailing up to my waist before squeezing. My heart soars in this one possessive moment.

His eyes meet mine and they speak words either of us are too afraid to share.

All I know is that his hands on me feel like home.

As if sensing my submission, his enormous hands squeeze me tighter, dwarfing my body and making me feel like his own personal doll.

"Fuck, Ashley. My dirty little treasure." His hands trail up my body as he rises to meet my face, his nose trailing the outline of my jaw before nipping my chin and finding my lips. "You're my damn weakness. My biggest temptation. My fucking demise."

In one rough movement, Titus' hands latch onto my ass seconds before his thick cock impales me for the very first time.

"Oh, gawd," I groan as my eyes roll to the back of my head. Stars. Glorious stars burst before me, all shrouded in darkness as my entire body vibrates against Titus.

There's no doubt in my mind that this is heaven and I never want to leave.

His delicious girth slams in and out of me, stretching me and rubbing me in all the right places. It's as if this man was made for me.

My own personal pleasure palace. I grin like a mad woman, because that's exactly what Titus has made me. A greedy little mad woman.

"Baby, you're so damn tight." Titus pants against the shell of my ear as my ass slams into the wooden door, bouncing off of it like a damned game of handball.

Growling, I bite at his jawline. "And you're so damn big."

I feel him pulsing inside of me, the sensation making my walls clench around his girth.

"Oh, fuck. Don't do that. Not if you don't want the first round to end so quickly." His tongue peeks out, licking a line up my neck before sucking the tender flesh into his mouth.

"First round? Oh, god. Yes, more, please." With my legs wrapped around his waist, I roll my hips and ride him, all while milking his pulsating cock.

Titus' hand reaches up to my neck, his fingers squeezing before letting go and pounding his fist against the door.

"Damn it." He groans before issuing a string of curse words.

I'd heard about this before, power play where choking is involved. The last thing I want is for him to hold back. Not only do I trust him, but I want to give him as much pleasure as he gives me.

He needs to know this.

"Titus," His eyes meet mine, hesitation lurking behind the beautiful orbs. "I'm yours, my body is yours. Touch me any way

30

you please."

His forehead presses against mine, our noses grazing against one another. "Why are you so damn perfect, *min skatt?*"

"I just am. Now fuck me. Fuck me hard."

Titus' lips violently clash against mine, cutting me off and devouring my mouth as if I were his last meal.

Yes, please.

My hips roll, chasing the delicious sensations as Titus slides in and out of me, our wet skin slapping together and creating a delicious cacophony of sounds.

His left hand grips onto my ass, meanwhile his right finds its way up to my neck. His fingers squeezing me tightly in a possessive hold.

In this moment, *I am his.*

That one movement seems to be our undoing.

Titus' eyes squeeze shut as he lets out a guttural roar, "Come with me. NOW!"

His right hand drops, reaching my clit and pressing the pad of his thumb against it, detonating my entire body into an explosion of pure bliss on command.

Yes, this is heaven, and I never want to leave.

Titus

"*Min skatt*, you're home." Brushing the hair out of her face, I see the woman she's become, the woman I could never let myself have.

"We're home?" She opens her eyes wide, taking in the guest

room in William's Highland Park home. "Oh my god, that's twice I've fallen asleep on you. You didn't have to carry me in here. I could've just walked if you'd woken me sooner. I'm so sorry. I feel like you've been doing nothing but taking care of me all night." Her whole body flushes as she looks away.

"Don't. Don't apologize for anything. I loved taking care of you and besides, you had a very thorough *workout*." I roll in my lips, trying to bite back a smile. "Not to mention, you'd already had an eventful day."

Her slender hand reaches up and caresses my jaw line, causing me to instinctively close my eyes and soak up every second of this moment.

"Stay with me tonight?" Her small voice coaxes my eyes open, and what I see is nothing short of frustrating.

Her eyes are pleading, begging me for something I cannot give. What I'd give to be that for her, be the man she needs.

Taking her hand in mine, I pull it from me. "I'm sorry, Ashley. I can't. I don't do cuddly." I know it's a dick thing to say, especially after everything she's been through. But in my experience, being honest is always the best policy. Leading her on would only make things worse.

Getting up from the bed I've just refused, I take in a deep breath and sigh. "Get some rest. You have a lot of decisions coming up and your brother will undoubtedly want to talk about whatever happened yesterday."

"Ugh, don't remind me." Ashley quickly pulls the covers over her head before lowering them just enough to peek through. "Please, don't tell him anything. I'm not ready to deal with him yet."

Bending at the waist, I lower myself and place a kiss on her forehead. "Whatever you want, little treasure. Sweet dreams."

Prying myself from her presence is even harder than I would have imagined now that I've tasted her. But just like a Band-Aid, the faster you yank it, the less painful it is.

Not giving myself one second longer, I retreat, unwilling to look back at what I've dared to taste but could never have.

Chapter Three

TITUS

The night air cools my heated skin, flustered from the whirlwind of emotions flowing through me. That shit gives me vertigo. And by *shit*, I mean emotions. Like a disease, I steer clear of anything having to do with catching feelings, and what just happened in that room—*in that airplane*—felt an awful lot like feelings.

I couldn't get out of that room fast enough. The longer I stayed, the harder it became to pull myself from her comforting touch and delectable body. Thankfully, every time I started to fall into her, visions of William finding us in bed together kept flashing through my mind, sending cold sweat running down my back.

What a fucking nightmare. I could see it all playing out now.

What would start out as a verbal assault would soon turn into physical blows, ending with either one of us six feet underground. Neither of us are known for backing down, and although I love him like a brother, I'm not sure I'd let him take me out like that.

No, there's no way in hell I could risk him finding out about my tryst with his sister.

A tryst. That's all it was. That's all it'll ever be.

A world where Ashley Hawthorne is mine doesn't exist. If she really knew what I was like, what monster lurks beneath, she wouldn't want anything to do with me.

William knows, he's seen it first-hand. If he ever found out about tonight...

My phone vibrates as I get into my blacked-out Escalade. Pulling it out of my pocket, the light illuminates my face of betrayal and I grimace.

"William, what can I do you for?"

"What can you do me for? What the fuck?" William chuckles into the line, no doubt wondering what the hell is wrong with me. "Well, for starters, you can tell me you got my sister home safe."

Sucking in a deep breath before answering, I squeeze my eyes shut as if the action could help me unsee Ashley writhing beneath me. "Yeah, brother. She's home safe. I have guards posted outside and you have your system in place. She's safe for the night."

"Good. I appreciate you going out to get her. You know I have my hands full with my crazy ex and Bella's case right now. Any clue what caused her to break down like that? The last time I heard she was that upset was... well, you remember. You were there."

"I remember, and she didn't say."

"You were with her for what, five hours? And she didn't say?"

"Look, you know I'm not the prying type. Especially when it comes to emotions. Just know that she was settled when I left her." I cringe, my stomach rolling at the way I left her—naked, flushed, and thoroughly fucked.

"Fine, fine. Yes, I acknowledge you're not a Chatty Cathy. Maybe I can get Bella to figure out what happened. If it was that boyfriend of hers, I'll have his head on a platter."

My throat tightens and breathing halts. "Boyfriend?"

"Yeah, you know the attorney she'd been dating for the past year? I'm sure I would have mentioned him before. He's a pretentious little fucker, and a social climber to boot."

"Must've missed it." More like blocked it out of my memory. The thought of Ashley with another man makes me see red. My grip tightens around the phone, the skin across my knuckles crackling as it expands.

"Anyway, I'm sure I'll find out soon enough. Thanks again, brother. I appreciate you going out to get her. I know she could have hopped on the plane alone, but from what you said, it sounded like she needed some support and we never leave a man behind... Or woman in this case."

"No worries. It was my pleasure."

"Alright, call me if anything changes."

"Ten-four." I press the 'end' button and throw my head back into the headrest.

What have I done? Not only did I take advantage of William's little sister when she was emotionally vulnerable, but it turns out I could have turned her into a cheater.

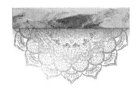

Ashley

What just happened?

It's been hours since Titus left my room, and I can't seem to make sense of what went down. I sit up after restlessly flailing in bed. There's no way I'm going to get any sleep.

Wrapping my arms around myself, I try to figure out what in the hell just happened.

One moment I'm bawling my eyes out for time wasted with my loser ex and the next I'm in the throes of passion with my dream crush only to be thrown off the cloud I was on and be slammed back onto earth with three little words. *'I don't do cuddly.'*

What the fuck? What does that even mean? Does he not do affection or is that his way of saying he doesn't do affection with me?

Do I even want a relationship after what Brad did to me?

There's a soft knock at my door, causing my heart to stutter. *Did Titus decide to come back?*

Giving myself a mental facepalm, I come to terms that this answers whether or not I want a relationship with Titus.

"Come in," I call out into the dark.

The door creaks open and a tall figure steps into the room, my heart sinking at the realization that it's just my brother.

"Hey, sis. I'm sorry to wake you, but there's been an emergency." William's down-turned mouth and furrowed brows have me hopping out of bed faster than the speed of light.

"What's the matter? Is Titus okay?"

William's brows lift to his hairline and it's then I realize that I've given myself away. "Yes, Titus is okay." His brows come back down and press together. "Is there a reason he wouldn't be?"

"No, it's just he's the last person I saw, so the first person to come to mind." God, I hope he buys this. "Anyway, tell me what's wrong? Is there anything I can do to help?"

"I'm glad you ask, because we will definitely need your help."

"We?"

Williams' hand reaches behind his neck, rubbing it slowly. "Yes, Aiden was injured while on a job and he's now in a coma. Bella didn't handle the news well, justifiably so. She lost her mother when she was fifteen and now her father..."

My hand flies up to my open mouth where I'm gasping for air. "Oh my god! That's horrible!"

My brother, William, and four other men are the original founders of the Men of WRATH, a national security firm. There's always the risk of injury, but nothing like this has ever happened before. Especially not to Bella's father, Aiden. He's a former Navy SEAL and assigned to the highest profile cases because of his skills and training.

"Yes. You know Bella has been helping me with Harper as well as caring for her own twin brothers, but I'm afraid she's not going to be able to keep up her nannying responsibilities right now. Aiden is being cared for at a top facility in California and we all fly out in a couple of hours. I was hoping you could help with the kids in the meantime. What do you say, Ash? Can you come with us to California?"

"Of course! Don't worry about the kids." I take his hands in mine and squeeze. "Anything for Bella. Poor girl must be distraught." My thoughts flashback to when I was interviewing her for the nanny position. We've seen her grow into the young lady she is today and something so tragic couldn't have happened to such a good person.

When her mother died, she took on the responsibility of caring for her two little brothers, carting them around from soccer to karate and foregoing whatever social life a girl her age would be accustomed to.

William's voice breaks me out of my thoughts. "Thank you. She's sleeping right now, but you know the kids' schedule."

"Say no more. I'll be up with them and getting them ready for the trip. What time do we fly out?"

"Nine in the morning. I've already arranged for the rental home where we'll be staying, and you'll have your own room and *en suite* there. I can't thank you enough for this. You're a lifesaver."

Looking deep into his eyes, I can see that he's really hurting, and I'm not sure if it's just for his friend Aiden or the nanny he's grown so fond of. A niggle tells me it might be a bit of both. "I'll always be here for you, and for Bella. Family is everything."

William gives me a small smile, "Yes. Family *is* everything. Speaking of family, what kind of a shit brother would I be if I didn't ask about what landed you back in Dallas. Tell me it wasn't that worthless boyfriend of yours."

Mayday, Mayday. Change of topic, ASAP. "Nothing you need to worry about right now. I promise we will talk about it when the time is right. You have a ton on your plate and my problems are nowhere near the level of tragedy that yours are."

"This isn't a competition, Ashley. You know I'm always here for you. I know I'm not as good as one of your girlfriends, but I'm family and I'll always have your back."

His sentiment brings tears to my eyes. God, if he only knew. But there's no way I could tell him, for if I tell him I risk divulging what transpired between his friend and me on that airplane.

Shaking my head, I sigh. "I know brother, but now is not the time."

He places a kiss on my forehead, "Whenever you're ready, I'm here."

I nod, unsure if there will ever come a time where I'll freely tell him what happened. Pushing him out the door, I whisper-shout, "Enough about me, go get some sleep. I doubt you've had any so far and we're leaving in a couple of hours."

"Yes ma'am." William chuckles as the door closes behind him.

Yeah, I doubt he'd be laughing if he knew what really happened with Titus and me. Groaning against the door, I let myself slide down to the floor.

What have you gotten yourself into this time, Ashley?

But as the memory of Titus sliding his thick fingers inside of me makes my lady parts clench, I can't bring myself to care.

Chapter Four
ASHLEY

It's too damn early.

I make my way to the kitchen with one eye open, one year old Harper on my hip and the twins in tow. The kids are lucky I love them so much or I wouldn't have agreed so readily.

Who am I kidding? William has always been there for me, acting more like a surrogate father than big brother. I'd never let him down.

Still. Coffee, then breakfast for the kids. Priorities.

I'm placing my mug under the built-in espresso machine, something I really appreciate about William's gourmet kitchen, when I hear a yawn behind me.

"We must be on the same wavelength because I'm in desperate

need of my java."

Whirling around, I almost whack poor Harper's head on the cabinet. "Oh my god, I thought it was just me and the kids." My head jerks toward the twins sitting at the breakfast bar.

Bella chuckles, but her soft smile does nothing to hide her swollen red eyes, "Sorry. Didn't mean to startle you. I'm usually up before them so this is me sleeping in." She shakes her head as her eyes go glassy. "Thank you for helping out. I'm still not sure how this is real life."

My free hand reaches out to squeeze her shoulder. "Of course. Always. You've been so good to our family, the least I could do is be here for you when you needed it."

Bella's face flushes as she looks away. "Yes, anyway. Go sit. I'll make us something quick to eat before we have to leave."

She doesn't have to ask me twice. I suck at cooking. My version of breakfast was going to be a toss-up between cereal and Pop Tarts.

Grabbing my coffee, I walk past her and plop myself and Harper right next to the boys. My niece, however, has a different idea. Wriggling out of my arms, she gets down and walks straight for Bella, holding up her arms.

"Mo-mma." Her little blonde curls bounce as she hops up and down, reaching toward a blushing Bella.

"Morning, pumpkin." She picks her up so effortlessly, like she was born to do this. "My name is Bella. B-e-l-l-a."

"Mo-mma." My niece giggles as she tugs on one of Bella's long black tendrils of hair.

"She's been doing that all week." Six-year-old Max mumbles with his mouth full of banana.

"I don't know where she got it from." Bella's cheeks are still a crimson shade and I can't help but smile.

"It must come naturally to her. You're the closest thing to an actual mother figure she has. Lord knows, her crackpot mother was never around, always handing her off to me whenever I was in town or pawning her off at that overpriced Mother's Day out program." I pull the mug to my lips with both hands as I stare on.

They really do look adorable together.

Too bad she's too young for William. And, god, if she knew our family secrets, she'd never agree to be with him anyway.

Speaking of the devil, William walks in as Bella is placing Harper in her high-chair, and it doesn't go unnoticed that his hand trails across her lower back as he walks by with his morning greetings.

Note to self, grill him later.

"Morning, Brother."

William jumps at the sound of my voice. Uh-huh. Definitely grilling him later.

"Morning, Ashley. I didn't see you there."

"That's funny, I'm right in the middle of the room. Guess your focus was elsewhere," I snicker into my mug.

"Probably on the million things we need to do once we land. Do you have everything packed?"

"Yes, I had my stuff packed last night and I helped the kids with their things this morning. We're ready."

"Great, the guys are waiting at the hanger. So as soon as we're done eating, we'll be heading out."

"The guys? They're all coming too?" I nibble on my lower lip, suddenly very nervous of the prospect of seeing Titus again. So soon and on the very plane we tasted each other for the first time.

My brother's face scrunches together, "Yes. It's natural for the team to want to see Aiden. We've been through so much together. We weren't about to let him go through this alone."

"Of course." My head repeatedly jerks up and down before I abruptly get up from my seat, heading to the sink, suddenly needing to do something with my hands in order to not self-combust.

I start washing the mug as I mentally psych myself up. Of course they'd want to see Aiden too. They're like a packaged deal.

William is the brains and business behind WRATH Securities. Then there's Aiden, the former Navy SEAL and head of Security. Ren is Aiden's little brother—a hacker by day and ladies' man by night. Fourth in their crew is Hudson, the money guy, he oversees the financials. And last but not least, Titus, who has investigative skills that could make the Pope shudder.

"Is there a problem with the men joining us?" William whispers behind me and I drop the mug that I'd been scrubbing this entire time.

The ceramic cracks inside the apron-front sink, sending shards of cream scattering in the basin.

"Damn, William. Way to sneak up on someone." Bella's soft chuckle comes from beside me and I can't help but startle.

"What is this? The Hawthorne house of Ninjas?"

Bella's slender arms reach into the sink, pulling out the broken mug piece by piece. "I guess I learn from the best." Her eyes dart up to my brother and there's no mistaking what I see there. It's the same way I've looked at Titus since I was fifteen. "He used to catch me off-guard all the time when I first started working here."

"Our security firm wouldn't be what it is today if we walked around like a town crier, now would it." William smiles down at her with a tenderness I've never seen before, other than for family, of course. That man dotes on his daughter like she's the end all be all—and I suppose that's how it should be.

Not that we learned that from our parents. Like William says, they'd make Peg and Al Bundy seem like parents of the year. Breaking their bubble, I pat William on the back. "Nope. And while you guys do your ninja stuff down here, I'll go get the kids' bags and meet you out front. I'm not a breakfast person anyway." Looking toward Bella, I thank her for helping me pick up the splattered shards and beeline it to the guest room, suddenly feeling the urge to freshen up a little more.

Gah. Were it any other man, I'd give a rat's ass if they saw me in my sweats and bird-nest messy bun.

But this is Titus.

My Dark Knight in shining armor.

Now that I know he sees me, *really* sees me, I gotta make him drool a little.

Chapter Five

ASHLEY

He won't look at me.

What the hell?

The man couldn't pry himself from between my thighs last night, and now he won't even spare me a damn look?

Oh, hell no. This will not fly.

It would be one thing if last night were a one-night stand with a damn stranger, but this is Titus. He's seen me at my most vulnerable, and I'm not talking about being naked and tied up.

I'd expect ghosting from anyone but him.

"Excuse me." I get up from my seat on the jet and move past William and Bella, heading toward the private bedroom.

William crinkles his forehead and raises his brows as he follows my movement. "Everything okay, sis?"

"Yup. Just left something of mine in the bedroom last night. I'm going to check to see if it's still there."

At my words, Titus chokes on his drink.

Uh-huh. Glad to see he's not oblivious.

Ignoring him, I keep walking straight into the comfortable sized room and sit on the bed. I didn't really leave anything in here but I'm not about to walk right back out.

I'm about to pull my phone out and play some solitaire—how fitting—when the door creaks.

"What the fuck are you trying to do? Get us killed?"

Looking up I see Titus and his normally stoic face, pained and a deep shade of red.

Rolling my eyes, I answer, "Relax. If anyone is giving anything away it's you, sneaking in here."

"I'm not giving anything away. Your brother is busy consoling Bella while the rest of the team tries to manage a hyper toddler." His body stalks forward, stopping just in front of me on the bed. "What did you forget? We were careful last night."

Just then I notice movement from his slacks. Holy shit. He's fully hard and I think I just saw his length twitch in his pants.

"Eyes, up here, little treasure." The asshole has the audacity to smirk at me.

"Didn't think you'd even remember last night." I whisper-hiss, narrowing my eyes. "The way you've been acting since I arrived at the hanger, one would question if we've even met before."

His hand jets out, grasping my jaw and gripping it tightly, our eyes locking on to one another. "Little girl, you know nothing. What would you have me do? Greet you with this?" His lips seek mine as they envelop me in their warmth and his tongue demands entry, needing its other half.

"Mmmmhmmmm," I moan into him. God, this never gets old. The feel of his velvety soft tongue caressing mine. The taste of cinnamon and cloves. The bruising grip of his hands on me. I want it all. Always.

His free hand grips me at the nape, pulling on my hair and tilting my head back, giving him further access and deepening our kiss.

I'm about to drop back onto the bed when suddenly, it's all gone. Just as fast and furious as it started, it's all ripped away.

Opening my eyes, I shake myself from this living dream and see a shocked Titus before me. His blue eyes are wide open, and his mouth is slack-jawed, meanwhile his hands are gripping at his hair like it were his lifeline.

"What happened?" My hand flies up to my bruised lips, trying to keep the sensation of his mouth on mine.

"Fuck, Ashley. This can't happen again." He arranges himself as the realization of what I am sets in.

I'm his dirty little secret. He doesn't really want me. Not in any way that matters.

My chest feels like it's being ripped wide open. The crevice this farce has left behind is so much worse than my cheating ex.

If I were being honest with myself, I never really loved Brad. He was the right guy, at the right time, from the right family. I knew he didn't want me for my money, he had his own. Everything was just... convenient, when it came to him.

But this?

This hurts so much worse. Titus has always been the unattainable. Never letting myself dream of what could be. But last night changed everything. Or so I thought.

I thought that he finally saw me. Saw me the way I see him. Like a partner. An equal. Someone to share things with.

I guess I was wrong. He didn't know what to do with a crying Ashley, so he shut me up the only way he knew how. Damn, he told me as much.

'Let me take care of you the only way I know how.' His words echo in my mind.

Ugh. How could I be so stupid! My heart aches and my eyes prickle with the promise of unshed tears.

Not wanting Titus to see what he's done to me, I quickly get up. Making sure there isn't a hair out of place and schooling my face into one of indifference, I walk past Titus, ready to rejoin the rest of the crew.

"Ash, wait." Titus reaches out and grabs my hand, but I jerk it away.

"No. You've made your intentions pretty clear. You don't want to make anyone think there's anything going on between us. Best we leave separately." I step out into the main cabin, not giving him the opportunity to respond.

I don't care if he wants to backtrack. I've had enough of men stomping all over me.

Needing to make myself a priority, I'll be damned if I let a man make me feel differently.

Even if it's the one who's haunted my dreams for the better part of my life.

Titus
Raw.
That's what I'd do if she were mine.

I'd spank her fucking ass raw.

Walking into the hotel room I've booked for the weekend, I let out a growl. This is not how I envisioned this trip going. I'm not sure what I was expecting, but it definitely wasn't what happened on the jet.

Doing a one-eighty, I turn my back to the bed and flop back. It's a nice enough suite, with its sleek artwork and modern furnishings, devoid of any warmth. No. This room is cold and stark, just like my bed tonight.

Pulling out my phone I see I've missed a call from Hudson. Dialing his number, I place the call on speaker.

"Hey. Finally! We've been trying to reach you." His exasperated tone comes through the line and I have to roll my eyes.

"Man, I just saw you downstairs in the lobby. What the hell could've happened in the last fifteen minutes?"

"Whatever. What's the point of having a phone if you always have it on silent?"

"Are you going to stop busting my balls and tell me what was so urgent?"

"Oh, yeah. William called and said we can't see Aiden until tomorrow. Something about limiting the number of visitors at the hospital. Anyway, we were thinking of heading over to that restaurant in Malibu. The one on the water. God knows we could all use a distraction, if you know what I mean."

My stomach knots and my throat gets tight. If the crew only knew what sort of distraction I gave Ashley last night, I'm not so sure they'd be inviting me on their outing right now.

I may not know what the hell happened between William's sister and me, but I do know one thing—I'm not ready to dip my wick in someone other than her.

The mere thought of it just feels wrong, like pineapple on a pizza.

"Titus? You there?" Hudson's voice brings me back to the conversation.

Trying not to sound *off*, I mentally shake myself from this fog. "Yeah, I'm here, brother. I'll pass on tonight. It's been a long day and I'm not really in the partying mood."

Hudson scoffs, "Neither are we. It's more of a mind-numbing diversion we're after, but I get it. This whole thing has been a mind fuck. It easily could've happened to any one of us, but for it to have happened to our most seasoned... well, that's just downright tragic."

I blow out a breath before responding, "You can say that again. Anyway, stay safe tonight. Call me if you guys need anything."

"Sure thing, brother."

And with a click of the line, I'm back to contemplating where the hell I went wrong.

Was it catching the eye of the forbidden fruit, my tasting it, or the fact that I've somehow led it on?

Whatever the case, I have about ten hours to figure it out before I see Ashley again, and something definitely needs to change.

We got lucky that nobody's noticed anything. But with the way she's throwing visual daggers at me, there's no doubt in my mind it won't be long before someone does.

And when they do, all hell will break loose.

ACTS OF GRACE

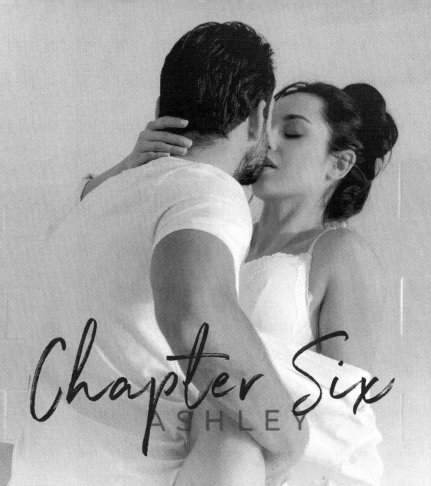

Chapter Six

ASHLEY

Talk about the worst sleep ever. Might as well have been sleeping on a pile of rocks.

Don't get me wrong, the rental home William found is absolutely stunning. The epitome of California *chic*, and my guest room is no different.

The king size bed has a massive cloud-like feather bed with extremely soft white bedding, but none of it did a damn thing to ease the turmoil in my brain and heart last night.

I'm coming out of the *en suite* bath, fluffing my wet hair with a bath towel when there's a soft knock on the door.

Looking at the clock I see it's only five in the morning, the kids won't be up for at least another hour and a half.

"Come in," I call out.

"Ashley, I'm so glad you're up." My brother comes in looking like I feel. He must've had a rough night too. "Bella wants to head out to the hospital in an hour and I'm going to drive her there. Just wanted to make sure you were up and had the monitors to the kids' rooms."

"Yes, to both. Hooked them up last night and had them charged and next to me the whole night. They've been out like a light." Blowing out a raspberry, I close my eyes. "Wish I could say the same."

William's hand reaches out squeezing my shoulder. "I know. This whole thing has been hard on all of us. We'll be visiting Aiden on a rotation schedule since there's limits on how many people can visit the intensive care unit he's in. The guys should be here later this morning doing research and working from the back office. We're setting up a home base of sorts until we know what the next move will be with Aiden's attackers. I'll call them when I know more so we can go over the visitation schedule."

William pulls me toward him, placing a kiss on my forehead. "Thank you. Seriously, Ashley. You're saving my ass once again."

Smiling up at my big brother, my heart fills up with pride. "Always. I know you'd do the same for me. You always have. Now go. I have to finish getting ready before the tiny dictators are up and harassing me for food." I chuckle, remembering their request for Bella's famous pancakes.

Bless their little hearts.

I'm the fun auntie, but I definitely won't be plying them with the equivalent of Bella's home cooking.

Not if they don't want to end up at the hospital from food poisoning.

My body shudders as I close the door. Flashbacks of the one time I tried to cook Thanksgiving dinner assault me.

Our parents had just passed and I wanted to do something special that would bring William and I closer, so I decided to cook.

Bad idea.

Let's just say we definitely became closer after taking turns praying to the porcelain god that night.

Ugh, never again.

"Ashley, you outdid yourself." Titus' eyes lock with mine as he picks up a piece of bacon from the breakfast spread on the kitchen island.

Meanwhile, Hudson snorts as he stuffs a slice of cantaloupe into his mouth. "You do know she didn't make any of this right? Girl would burn water if it were possible."

Flinging a dish towel at Hudson, I growl, "Hey! I ordered everything. That has to count for something right?"

Heat creeps up my face and I don't dare look at Titus. I mean, I grew up with these guys so it's no surprise that I'm no Susie Homemaker. My mother never taught me and we always had a hired chef so there was never a need.

"Dumb ass." Titus smacks Hudson upside the head. "That's no way to treat the woman who's hosting your voracious ass. Be glad she decided to feed you. You know she didn't have to."

Hudson gives him the side-eye as he takes his seat at a barstool. "Sorry, Ashley. Meant no disrespect."

"No worries. No offense taken. I'm used to your ways." I wink at Hudson and hear a little growl from Titus.

Interesting. Is that jealousy?

Plugging my phone into the wall charger, I mentally prepare myself. It's been off for the past thirty-six hours and I have no doubt my ex has left me numerous messages.

The vision of him running after me the other night makes my stomach want to revolt.

"Do we know when our visiting hours will be up?" Titus asks as he sips his coffee.

"William said he'd call." Waving my phone toward the room, it decides to come to life, and the incessant dings start coming through, one right after the other.

"Damn, someone's blowing you up. Is it William?" Hudson's eyes narrow in concern, but turning to look at Titus, his expression is something completely different.

His face is scrunched up as if pained, meanwhile his eyes are narrowed, conveying a mixture of sadness and anger. *What the hell?*

Looking down at my phone, I confirm what I already know. "No, it isn't William. It's some asshole who can't take a hint."

I place my phone on silent before stepping away and grabbing a mug out of the cabinet.

"Hey, you sure you should be doing that?" Hudson calls out and I whirl around to see what he's talking about. The twins are in the playroom and Harper is in her high-chair so she can't be getting into trouble.

With furrowed brows, I inspect the room. That's when I see it.

Titus scrolling through my phone.

"Mind your own business, Hudson," Titus spits out as he

scrolls through my device.

"Excuse me? What do you think you're doing?" I slam my empty coffee mug on the counter next to Titus, but the asshole doesn't even flinch.

"Ummm, I'll take Harper into the playroom with the boys. I think she wants to see me beat their little smug behinds on Mario Kart." Hudson awkwardly slides out of his seat and heads toward Harper. "I think your auntie and Titus need to figure shit out."

He boops my niece on the nose as both Titus and I admonish, "Language!"

"At least you two can agree on something." Titus rolls his eyes as he picks little Harper up and walks away. "Don't think I didn't notice the tension between you two on the jet last night."

My jaw drops as I gape at them exiting the room, unable to form words.

"Ignore him. He won't say anything. I'll make sure of it." Titus' deep voice brings me back to his current transgression—hacking into my phone.

"He's not the one I'm mad at right now." My eyes narrow as I shove a finger into his chest, his very firm and toned chest. "Are you going to tell me how you got into my phone without my passcode?"

Without any trace of remorse, Titus looks me dead in the eyes. "I know all of your pass codes. For fucks sake, you haven't changed them since high school. You should really look into updating them."

My mouth hangs open for the second time this morning. "Excuse me? How can you say that so nonchalantly? That's my privacy. What business is it of yours whether or not I decide to change my pass codes or not?"

Titus puts down my phone and backs me against the counter, caging me in with his strong arms. "You forget one thing, *min skatt*. On more than one occasion, your brother has tasked me with caring for you. I take that duty very seriously." His face lowers to mine, our noses brushing against one another, breathing each other in. "You are mine to protect and I'll do what I see fit as long as it ensures one thing. Your safety."

I blink, unable to think clearly through this haze of lust that's suddenly come over me. Having him this close is dangerous.

"Okay. Explain to me how going through my phone is helping you keep me safe, because from where I'm standing it seems more like an invasion of privacy than a safety ploy."

His lips turn up on one side and it takes everything in me not to rise up to my tippy toes and lick that sensual mouth.

"And how do you like your current point of view?" His eyes are trained on my mouth, his thick fingers reaching up and pulling my lower lip free from the assault of my teeth.

I revel in the feeling of his rough thumb stroking my lip back and forth—hypnotized by the movement I almost forget what started this in the first place.

"No." I push him away, or try to. The man is built like a steel post. "You don't get to change the subject and try to distract me. Answer the question. Why are you looking through my phone?"

Pushing himself off from the counter, he groans into his palm and walks away. "Damn it, Ash. Why didn't you tell me you had a boyfriend?"

The air is sucked from my lungs and I stand there, flailing like a fish out of water. "What? Oh my god. Is that what this is all about? God, no!" I shriek while running toward him, turning his body once I've reached him. "I don't have a boyfriend. Not as of thirty-six hours ago, anyway. I caught him red-handed with another woman. Also, there may have been some chicken-noodle soup involved." I smile to myself remembering their shocked expressions as noodles and broth ran down their foreheads.

Titus tilts his head to the side and purses his lips, "Do I want to know?"

Closing my eyes, I let out a breath. "Ugh. I feel like such an idiot. I don't know how I didn't see the signs. Maybe it was because I really wasn't invested."

Bringing both hands to my face, I groan.

"Shhh. All that matters is that you're free from that jack-ass." Titus envelops me in his arms, and presses his palms to my back, rubbing up and down. "I'm sorry."

Peeling my face from his chest, I look up. "For what? Going through my phone?"

"Ha! No. I'm not sorry about that at all." He presses a kiss to the top of my head. "I'm sorry for taking advantage of such a tender situation. I shouldn't have let us go that far, little treasure."

"Don't." I shove at him, trying to break free from his hold, but he isn't budging. "I'm a grown woman and I knew what I was doing. I wanted everything you gave me. I wanted *you*."

Titus sucks in a sharp breath, his arms dropping from my body as if I were on fire. "Don't say that, Ash. You don't know what you're saying."

My brows drop and eyes narrow. "I know exactly what I'm saying. Seems to me like you're the one who isn't sure of things. One minute you're all over me and the next you're dropping me like a hot potato."

Titus' lips press into a grimace as he shakes his head. "I'm just trying to keep you safe. I've always wanted to keep you safe.

And you and me? That would only end in nothing but disaster."

My eyes narrow into tiny slits as my heart threatens to shatter. I've had enough of this push and pull, staying in front of him any longer will have me either stabbing him with a kitchen knife or me breaking down into a puddle of tears.

Choosing self-preservation, I walk toward the charging cellphone, yanking it from the wall. "Well, you can start by fucking off and staying the hell away from me and my phone."

Exiting the kitchen, I head to my room, needing a moment to gather myself before I tend to the kids.

I'm hanging on by a thread as it is, and it's a damn miracle my self-esteem hasn't gone and jumped off a cliff by now.

Good thing I know what I bring to the table, and honey, my cup runneth over.

ACTS OF GRACE

Chapter Seven
TITUS

Well, that went about as well as a brick to the head.

Do I go after her?

Fuck, I don't know. I think I've messed up enough for a lifetime. I should've known better than to go there with William's little sister.

I sigh as my pocket vibrates. Whatever just happened will have to wait to be resolved. *If that's even possible.*

"Titus. I can't reach Ashley. Is everything okay?" William's voice sounds panicked, and I can't help but feel a sucker punch to the gut.

"She's probably in the bathroom or something. I'm still in the kitchen and she stepped out. Hudson is in the playroom with the kids. Is everything okay?"

"Yes. I was just calling to give you the visitor hours. But I'm glad

I caught you instead of Ashley."

My hand squeezes the back of my neck, rubbing out the tension this whole situation has caused. "Oh? Why is that?"

"I tried talking to her last night about whatever happened in Florida, but she won't say. I know she's probably worried about me and all I have going on, but I don't want to be a shit brother."

"Okay. But what does that have to do with me?" I have a feeling I know what he's about to ask and I already think it's a terrible idea.

"I don't exactly have time right now, but I was hoping you could help out with her. Keep an eye out and maybe do a little digging."

"You sure she'd be okay with us poking around in her personal life? Last I checked, women aren't keen on their privacy being violated." Groaning inwardly, I can't help but feel like a hypocrite. My ass was rummaging through her phone not ten minutes ago like some jealous psycho lover.

"I know. I know. But what's a brother to do when she won't open up?"

"Fine." I run a hand across my face. This isn't going to be easy. I'm already having a hard time acting like a normal human being around her.

All I want to do is take her over my shoulder and take her to bed, lavishing her with my tongue and cock all day long.

"Thank you, brother. I knew I could count on you. Ren is mourning what's happened to Aiden and Hudson, he's dealing with his own shit."

"So what you're saying is I was your last hope." I chuckle into the line. Just as well. I couldn't handle someone else poking around in Ashley's personal life.

William laughs, for the first time in a long while and I'm glad

I was able to bring him a moment of levity amidst his chaos. "No. I mean, you *are* the only one available. But for some reason, whenever it comes to my sister, it always comes down to you being the one that's there for her. I couldn't have hoped for a better friend to help keep her safe."

Another dagger of guilt sinks deep into my chest. "Of course, brother. That's what family is for."

"Great. We'll talk more when you get here at eleven. You, Ashley, and Hudson will be part of the second visitation shift."

"Alright. See you later."

The line goes dead and I'm left holding the phone in a death grip.

I doubt he'd be feeling the same about me if he knew what transpired last night.

Well, on the bright side, now I have a semi-legitimate reason for having hacked into Ashley's phone.

Who cares if William's request might not be retroactive. Right?

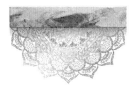

"You're just going to ignore me the entire time? That's very mature." My hands grip around the steering wheel, the squeaking of leather echoing my displeasure at Ashley's attitude.

"Don't. Now is not the time." Her head flings back to the twins and Harper strapped into the two rows behind us.

We've just left the hospital and I've been tasked as chauffeur. Never in my life did I think I was going to be driving a Dad-Mobile. Granted, it's a Suburban, so at least it's cool.

"The twins have their headphones on, playing their games, and Harper doesn't really understand what's going on. Spare me." I let out a breath at this infuriating woman. "So are you done ignoring me now?"

"I wasn't ignoring you. I was giving you the space you wanted. You made that clear on the jet and you made it even clearer in the kitchen."

We've had a rough morning, and the situation with Aiden was just downright depressing. I'm not in the mood for arguing, least of all with a woman who's driven my thoughts right off the brink of sanity.

"I don't want to fight with you, Ashley. This has been a highly emotional couple of days for us. Can't we call a truce?"

Her head jerks back violently as if I've slapped her. "Truce? You want to call a damn truce?"

My eyes narrow as I look over toward her, what's got her riled up now? "Yes, a truce. You know? No more fighting or bickering or whatever it is going on between us."

A tiny voice speaks up behind us, jerking us from our bubble. "It's called sexual tension."

I just about swerve out of the damn road. "Say what? Max, you're what? Seven? how in the world do you know what that is?"

"I don't know what it is, but I heard Hudson say you two needed to either fight it out or get a room. Your sexual tension was wrecking his vibe. What does sexual mean?"

I bust out into a violent coughing fit. Oh, hell no. I did not sign up for this shit.

"Um, Ashley?" I defer to her. She's got to be a million times better than me when it comes to this sort of thing.

"Hudson doesn't know what he's talking about. You know he

probably skipped out on his meds." Her lips press together as she glowers at me. "And that word isn't something you need to worry about. Not for a very long time."

I mouth a silent thank you to her. Handled like a true champ. No way I could've escaped that scenario without causing lifelong childhood scarring.

Her eyes narrow, but her lips curl up into a smirk. She mouths me a 'you're welcome' and my chest fills with warmth.

Things might not be as dire as I thought. Maybe I could still salvage our friendship.

Friendship.

The word doesn't sound right to me. She isn't just a friend. There's no way in hell I could stand to see another man lay claim to her.

I'd lose my damn mind.

"So. Are you done talking to that tool in Florida, or has he tried to reach out to you since this morning?"

Ashley's head whips toward me, "Excuse me? What gives you the impression that any of that is your business?"

"Your brother made it my business when he asked me to look after you."

"William did what?!" Ashley's pitch reaches unheard of heights as she stares daggers at me.

Flicking my eyes back to the road, I try and act cool even though I just threw my man under the bus. Unintentionally, but still.

It's as if this woman has me under a spell. For the past two days I've been in a fog. Acting before thinking.

"Answer me, Titus."

"Let's get inside first. Then we can talk." I roll into the driveway of the rental home and as soon as I place the car in park, the twins are unbuckling themselves as they race to the door.

"Fine but this isn't over. Not by a long shot."

I watch Ashley get out of the car and retrieve Harper from the back. Watching how tender she is with her niece makes my heart squeeze.

Visions of her swollen with child flash before me and I stumble back.

What the fuck?

Shaking that shit off, I lock the car and follow everyone inside.

"You're following me to the playroom. Don't think you're off the hook."

Biting my lip, I can't help but smirk at her feisty attitude. She's so damn cute being all authoritative. If she only knew that in my world, it's all about control.

Visions of Ashley clad in black leather and lace has my cock twitching in my slacks.

Her eyes don't miss the movement and her face flushes that beautiful shade of pink I love so much.

Am I ashamed of what her body does to mine? *Hell no.*

Do I get amusement from her noticing said reaction? *Hell yes.*

Closing the door behind me, I get my first view of the infamous playroom the twins love.

I see why. This place is heaven for a kid. Massive screen with multiple game consoles line one wall, to the right is a full bar complete with popcorn and snack machines. To the left is a toddler play area with climbing toys and plush lovies. Everything in the room is tied together with a massive sectional anchoring the room.

The twins claim the sectional, meanwhile Harper toddles over to the plush toys and doll house.

"Here." Ashley pats a chaise in the back of the room, calling me to her.

There she is again. Making demands.

If she were mine, I'd have to punish her for that.

"Okay. I'm here. What did you want to know?" I sit back, opening my arms wide along the backside of the seat.

"What did my brother ask you to do and why you?" Her voice comes out hesitant, like she's all of a sudden shy.

"First and foremost, you have to know he loves you and always wants what's best for you. With that said, he's just wanting to make sure you aren't forgotten in the chaos of the current events of our family. He's got a lot going on with his divorce, Aiden, and Bella's case. It's a lot to juggle, so naturally he asked me to help."

Her eyes narrow, some of that fire igniting behind those big blue eyes. "Okay, but why you?"

My hand reaches out, cupping her face and lifting it toward mine. "*Min skatt*, would you rather it be anyone else?"

Her quick intake of breath and dilating pupils draw my face closer.

"No." Her whispered admission sends shockwaves of pleasure through me, like her words are directly tied to my body. "No one but you."

Our faces are a breath away, drawing me even closer as our noses caress in the softest of touches.

Without thinking, my tongue comes out to play, licking her juicy bottom lip.

"Are you going to kiss her?" Matt's tilted head and inquisitive voice pulls me from bliss, meanwhile Ashley jumps back as if I've electrocuted her.

"What's up, little man? Need something?" I ask him because Ashley is still recovering from having been caught.

"Yeah, I was going to ask when we can see Dad again."

"My sweet boy!" Ashley, having gathered herself, pulls Matt into her. "I know this is all so new, but I promise we will be back first thing tomorrow morning. How about we order some pizza now and play a game together. Sound good?"

"Sounds good." Matt nods into Ashley's embrace, meanwhile she looks over his head at me with eyes that hold a sea of sadness.

There's no doubt she's currently fighting her own demons. Having to build herself up after what that dick of a man did to her. She's a fighter, my treasure. Always picking herself up and lifting others with her while she does it.

In that one definitive moment I make up my mind.

I vow to remove all sorrow from her heart. Even if it's only in my limited capacity.

I will not rest until her heart is whole and my little treasure is shining in all her splendor.

ACTS OF GRACE

Chapter Eight
ASHLEY

It's been a week since I last saw Titus.

One week since he said he'd be watching out for me in place of my brother, yet I've not seen his face or heard his voice once.

"What's up with you?" Bella's lips are pursed into a half-smirk. "You look like someone peed in your Cheerios."

Trying for a diversionary tactic, I change the subject altogether. "All of the kids are down for a nap—*at the same time*. Can you believe it?!" I sit next to her at the kitchen island, praying she doesn't go poking into my mood again.

"Ha! You've managed to bag a unicorn." She reaches over, patting my shoulder as her eyes fall to my earrings. "I've been meaning to tell you, I found one of your earrings back at the house in Dallas. It's really pretty and I'm sure you've missed it. It's a gold leaf with a black pearl in front of the stud backing."

My brows push together as I try and remember. "Huh, that doesn't sound like anything I own." Something akin to hurt and jealousy flash behind her grey orbs. *Interesting.* "Bella, is everything okay?"

"Yeah. Sure, of course. Why wouldn't it be? I was just thinking about the boys' birthday party coming up. I'm designing some of the party decor as well as the invites." She swivels her laptop toward me, showing me her work. "Do you think the other members of WRATH will come for their party?"

Surely this will pull the illusive Titus out of hiding. He doesn't miss out on holidays or parties. Never has and I doubt he'd start now. "I know Titus will be out here... visiting Aiden of course." My cheeks flush red. Why on earth would I be a keeper of that man's schedule. "I'm sure they'll all be coming back up here at one point or another, so why not just make it one big scheduled visit as opposed to various individual ones. That way we can pen in the boys' party."

William walks into the kitchen, heading for the fridge, and I'm glad this awkward exchange has been interrupted.

"Hey." My brother's deep voice rumbles in greeting.

Turning toward Bella I see her eyeing him like he's a prime rib special at our favorite restaurant. Uh-huh. I definitely need to look into this some more.

Not because I'm a Nosy Nellie, but because this could only spell disaster if she didn't really know about our family history.

Bella turns toward me, undoubtedly feeling my gaze as her pink face would indicate. Slamming her laptop shut she gets up from her stool. "I'm beat. Going to see if I can lay down for a bit while the kids are napping."

As soon as she's cleared the threshold to the hallway, William attacks. "What were y'all talking about?

I roll my eyes, "The twin's birthday party and whether or not the team will be able to make it out here." Pursing my lips, I press on. "She did, however, get really weird when she asked me about a missing earring she'd found at your house. She got this strange look on her face when I told her it wasn't mine. It almost looked like jealousy."

I like Bella, and the last thing I want is for her to get hurt. If she is getting mixed up with my brother, I think she's in for a world of pain.

"I wonder what that was about." William shrugs as he takes a big swig from the orange juice container. *The man doesn't even like orange juice.*

"Hmmmm." My eyes flick between the jug and him. "You know it would be a terrible idea for you to hook up with her, right? She's thirteen years younger than you. *Thirteen.*" The words taste like chalk in my mouth. Here I am, giving my brother shit for something I'm guilty of doing myself. I'm only three years older than Bella, making me a decade younger than Titus. Titus, who also happens to be William's friend. Looking up at the ceiling, I go for broke on my hypocritical tirade. "Not to mention she's your best friend's niece and friend's daughter. A friend who's in a coma. Oh, and let's not forget that you have a deranged ex who won't let you go. Do you really want to bring her into that mess?"

God, I hate playing the devil's advocate. I'm never a cock-block, but someone needs to look out for Bella. I don't want her getting run over when the truth comes out. Because let's face it, darkness always gives way to light, and the truth always comes out.

William slams the fridge door. "There's no bringing her into anything because there is nothing going on between us."

I scoff. There's not a snowflake's chance in hell I believe what he's saying. "Brother, all of those reasons don't even come close to touching what the real problem would be. The whole situation between our parents is the big whopper and what should be your biggest deterrent. Does she know about our dad? That's all sorts of fucked up." I shake my head and close my eyes, willing the memories away. "If Bella were to find out, she may never want to speak to you again. Do you really want to risk building a relationship only to have it fall apart on you? You'd have that big secret looming over you at all times. Waiting for the other shoe to drop."

"What big secret?" Bella asks as she steps back into the kitchen.

William's head jerks toward the sound of her voice. "I thought you were going to take a nap."

"I forgot my charger." Bella raises a brow as she picks up the laptop charger still attached to the outlet under the kitchen island. "So, what's the big secret?"

Pulling a Titus, William goes from casual to dick in two seconds flat. "My father's death. As you can see, it's none of your concern; and if it's all the same to you, I'd rather not talk about it."

Poor Bella is caught off-guard by his emotional whiplash, "I-I'm so sorry. I had no idea."

Regret swims in William's eyes as he gives her a curt nod and walks away. "Mhm. I'll be in the study."

Grabbing Bella's hand in mine, I give it a squeeze. "You didn't do anything wrong. I promise. He just has a lot of decisions weighing on him."

She gives me a timid smile, her eyes downcast. "You're probably right. I should try and get some rest before the kids are up. It's a miracle they're still down."

"Hey, Bella?" I call to her as she walks away.

"Yeah?" She looks back, her sad eyes full of light.

"Let's have some girl time soon. You're an amazing woman and I'd like to be friends if that's okay with you." I laugh, thinking of all the fake friends I've made along the way. "It's so hard to find kindhearted genuine people. All the friends I had back in Florida were phonies and the girls in Dallas... well, let's just say the circle we run in is vicious."

Bella lets out a snort. "Oh my god. You can say that again. The Dallas elite is really just a civilized pack of hyenas. Waiting for the next carcass to drop so they can pounce." She purses her lips and smiles. "So, yes. I would love a girls' night."

I clap my hands together, smiling from ear to ear. "Okay, just let me know when and I'll make sure we get the guys to watch the kids."

"Hah! I'd pay money to see that." Bella lets out a giggle as she walks into the hallway.

She really is such a lovely person. I definitely wouldn't be opposed to her becoming family, as long as my brother came clean about our history.

It's the hiding of secrets that really irks me.

Like my ex. The fucking asshole didn't have the decency to tell me he wanted more than what our relationship offered.

Nope, he chose to go outside of our arrangement for some extracurricular fun.

Arrangement. That's exactly what that relationship was. Sure, I had moments of happiness, and I even grew attached to the comfort of having a partner.

Thinking back, I was more so in love with the idea of settling down, having a stable relationship and someone to count on. But let's be honest, that was all fake. There wasn't a moment of truth involved in my life. From the fake friends who all knew Brad was going around behind my back, but never said anything to my face, to the Dallas debutantes who line my address book. *That stops now.* No more investing in worthless relationships. I don't have time for that shit.

Groaning into my hands, I turn my phone and look at the million-and-one messages I've received from Brad.

Hovering over the button, my finger reluctantly presses Play.

Baby, I'm sorry. It was a mistake. Please let me make it up to you.

Next.

Baby, please pick up the phone. I've been trying to reach you but the line goes straight to voice mail.

Next.

Baby, she meant nothing to—

Next.

I'm so sorry. Please, I'll never see her—

Next.

Ashley. Stop being a bitch. Mistakes happen. I'm giving you some space because that's clearly what you want right now, but this isn't over.

There he is. The real Brad. "Well, good luck trying to reach me, asshole. I'll be avoiding you like the bubonic plague." I roll my eyes at my phone as I turn the damn thing off.

"Who's the bubonic plague and is that today's equivalent of

cooties?"

My eyes flick up at the masculine voice, "Hudson?" My breath catches when I see he's not alone.

Titus stands stoically behind the playful Hudson, such a stark contrast to the void expression on Titus' face.

"How did you two get in here? I didn't hear the doorbell." My face flushes and voice pitches like a schoolgirl, caught off-guard by her crush.

Titus steps in front of Hudson, "The guards let us in. So, are you going to answer Hudson's question? Who is the bubonic plague and why are you wanting to stay away from them?" His cold eyes caress me with a violent sweetness. The combination of the two contrasting emotions creating a kink in my armor, lowering my defenses.

Unfortunately for him, I quickly remember our last interaction and how he's not spoken to me in over a week. "That's none of your concern. You should know better than to eavesdrop."

With a raised brow and a smirk, Titus walks closer. His frame looms over mine as he lowers his mouth to the shell of my ear and whispers, "Careful, little treasure. If you speak to me like that again, I'll be forced to spank that attitude out of you."

My body shudders, remembering the delicious sting his hand can bring, but it's the deep growl in his voice that has my panties soaking wet.

"You two need to get a room already." Hudson rolls his eyes as he raids the fridge. "We came to see William about some new info your lover boy uncovered."

"He is not my lover boy," I quickly spit out, embarrassed by the term he's awarded Titus. Needing to gain some distance from both men, I volunteer to fetch William. "I'll go get him. I was heading out anyway, so I'll be out of your hair."

Titus' eyes narrow and his mouth begins to open. Before he can say anything, I hold up a hand. "I'm going to the store and no I'm not meeting anyone. Security will be with me so there's no need for anyone else to come."

Titus' face puckers as if he's just taken a bite out of a lemon, meanwhile Hudson chuckles. "Told you, brother. You shouldn't have gone through her phone. Now you're going to have to really beg for it."

"Shut your mouth, Hudson. Don't make me remind you of your promise."

Shaking my head, I walk away from my biggest temptation. Listening to the two WRATH men verbally spar only serves as a reminder that whatever fantasy I concocted in my head could never be, no matter how bad I wish it so.

ACTS OF GRACE

Chapter Nine
TITUS

After a couple of minutes of giving Hudson the silent treatment, William struts in looking like a deflated balloon.

Hudson doesn't miss it either, "Uh-oh. Why the long face? Your ex giving you problems again?"

William groans as the heels of his palms rub his closed eyes. "Ugh. Does that woman ever stop giving me problems? Surprisingly, though, my mood has nothing to do with Heather and everything to do with a nosy sister."

My forehead crinkles. Ashley is many things but nosy isn't one of them. "What happened?" My voice comes out sounding gruff even to my own ears.

"Nothing. Don't pay attention to me. Anyway, have you dug up anything on why she high-tailed it to Dallas last week? Was it that cheating bastard, Brad?"

"Seems to me like the pot is calling the kettle black." Hudson singsongs before taking a bite of the massive turkey sandwich he unapologetically made himself.

I smirk, the man has a point, but it's not in my best interest to agree right now.

I've come up with a plan on the fly, something to get me closer to Ashley and figure out if that asshole is still trying to get her back.

"Last I checked, Brad stopped calling yesterday. He's been ringing her non-stop trying to win her back but then went off-grid all of a sudden. Very unusual for a man at his level of society. Not only that, but I have an inkling that there's more to this man than meets the eye. Everything about him and how he came into Ashley's life seems… convenient. Way too convenient." I fill William in on the news as I try and sound as calm as possible even though this whole situation has me feeling murderous. Last thing I want is for William to take over this job and handle the situation himself.

Being the control freak that I am, I don't trust anyone with Ashley's safety—not even her brother.

I mean, you can't blame me. So much has happened in the last couple of months, from Bella getting attacked, to William's ex having some sort of supernatural hold over the divorce judges. I'm not taking any chances that Ashley's well-being falls between the cracks.

Clearing my throat, I make my demand clear, "I've got a solid lead on what could be the problem with Brad. I'd like to shadow her for a bit and see if the target tries to reach out again. We can't be too safe, especially with what we've uncovered in Bella's case."

Williams' arm reaches the space between us and his hand pats me on the back. "Thank you, brother. You're right. I definitely don't want to drop my guard, especially with Ashley. I knew I could count on you."

My stomach recoils at that. God, if he only knew what I've done to his sister. "Great, I'll get started today as long as you don't need me here. Hudson has some new info he needs to go over with you."

"Yea! We have an email address for the person going back and forth with the judges. Seems like there might be a reason why they've all sided with your ex." Hudson speaks excitedly, forgetting that he has a mouth full of deli meat and cheese.

William's eyes widen comically and his brows practically hit his hairline. "What!? Well why didn't you say so?! Let's head to my study, and Titus, keep me posted on Ashley. I want to know what's going on and what we can do to keep that fucker, Brad, away."

Cocking a brow, I give him a solemn nod. "You've got it."

Trust me, there's nothing more I'd rather do than keep the fucktwad far away from my little treasure.

A man who cheats is not worthy of Ashley.

Scratch that. No man is worthy of Ashley.

Not even me.

Especially not me.

Ashley

I'm closing the door to my rental car when the passenger door flings open and a very serious Titus slides in.

"Excuse me?" I scoff.

"You're excused."

"That wasn't a literal question, Titus."

His brows raise and a slow smile graces his luscious lips. "Wasn't it?"

Blowing out a raspberry, I scowl. "What are you doing in the car, Titus? I thought I made it very clear I didn't want company."

"I heard you, but this is a new city. It's not safe for you to be prancing around." He flails his hands as if doing so will somehow make this ritzy part of California all of a sudden turn into a mafioso infested bordello.

"I never thought I'd have to tell you this, but did you forget that I'm the kid sister to WRATH securities? There's no way in hell I could ever go anywhere without someone watching my back. Ever since I came home, William has been playing the overprotective brother to a tee."

Titus growls, "If only the pathetic team in Florida had gotten the same memo."

My eyes narrow. "In Florida? What are you talking about? I thought I only had a team for special occasions there. William has always kept a detail on me. Even before you guys formed WRATH, but it was never as extensive as it is now… or was it?"

Letting out a sigh, Titus presses himself against the headrest. "I don't know why William hasn't told you about this, but seeing how he's placed me in charge, I think you need to be in the loop."

"Okaaay." There's something in his tone that sends a lead ball straight into my gut.

"You know why Bella is living with William now, right?" His hand reaches over and pries one of mine from the steering wheel.

"Yes. Bella had someone trash her car, and with Aiden being away for work, everyone thought it safer for her to stay with someone from the team. It made sense for her and the twins to stay with William since she was caring for my niece, Harper."

Titus' lips roll inward, his mouth forming into a thin line as he nods. "Mhm. But there's more. We think the person who did it is the same person who killed your father. The gun used on your father was the same gun used to shoot out Bella's tires."

My free hand flies up to my hand as I gasp for air. "Oh my god. The same gun!?"

"One and the same. We aren't sure why or how the two incidents are linked yet, but we aren't taking any risks." His eyes look past me, the color going from a light aqua to a dark indigo. "*This* is why you've always had a detail. And now that we have even more to worry about, there's no way in hell your brother wouldn't want you covered at all times."

Memories of my father's body flash before me and I shudder. The sick monster who did that to him is still free, and despite my brother's extensive security team, they've yet to locate the person behind Dad's violent and tragic death. It's as if they've vanished, never to be brought to justice.

Titus' face is full of sadness as his hand caresses my tear-stained face. "Shhh, min skatt. I've got you. Always have. Always will."

He repeats those words he's whispered once before, forever embedding themselves into my heart.

There's so much I don't know about this man and there's nothing I wouldn't give to make the darkness in him go away.

I don't know what's caused it but I sure as hell know I need it gone.

My free hand reaches over, caressing the rough stubble across his strong jawline. "Talk to me Titus, what's really got you worried."

"You." His voice comes out thick and husky, but his words have me blinking twice.

"Me? What about me?" I'm about to pull my hand away when he grabs it with one of his bringing it to his lips and kissing it softly.

"You. I worry about you getting swept up in the chaos, becoming a casualty of whatever this psychopath has in store." He plucks my index finger, gently nipping at the pad. "I worry that your dumb-as-fuck ex will somehow manage to win you back and drag you back to Florida."

"Me?" My breath hitches, as I try and take in a breath. The intensity of his stare paired with the sensual actions his mouth is playing on my hands has me at a loss.

"You." Titus sucks in my index finger, swirling it around in his warm mouth, the velvety feel of his tongue reminding me of all the naughty things it can do.

The pop of my finger being released from his mouth echoes through the stillness of the car.

His eyes find mine and it's as if we're caught in each other, unable or unwilling to move.

In one swift movement Titus reaches across, wrapping his thick hands around my waist and hoisting me over the center console. I groan as soon as my dress rides up and my aching core lands positioned right over his steel length.

"The feeling is mutual, little treasure." Titus' skilled hands travel up my body, ending tangled up in my hair. Our lips clash together in a violent and needy kiss, starving for one another. Nothing feels close enough.

Rolling my hips, I start to build that delicious friction which promises a sweet release. My hands reach down, trying to undo his belt but one of his hands stops me, his grip tightening around my wrist.

"Ashley." His voice is hoarse, my name sounding like a plea from his mouth. "As much as I want to impale you with my cock right now," his eyes flicker back to the house. "It's probably not a good idea to start something we can't finish. If William—"

My body shudders at the sound of my brother's name. "Enough of William. He doesn't own me and last I checked I was a grown-ass-woman who can do whatever she wants." Cupping Titus' face in my hands, I cock a brow and smirk. "Are you telling me that the strong and domineering Titus is afraid of doing whatever he wants?"

His eyes grow cold and I feel a sudden shift within the cabin. Dropping my hands, my face tilts toward the window. "I see. You don't want me. At least not enough for it to matter."

My chest aches as a tear I had no idea I was harboring rolls down my cheek. I'm about to open the car door when Titus' hand grips my face, bringing it to his, punishing my lips with a bruising kiss.

His free hand goes to my back and presses me into him as he juts his length into me, letting me feel just how much he wants me.

Moaning into his mouth, I feel electrified, my whole body tingling with euphoria.

"I want you more than I want air." His voice rumbles as his lips trace down my neck, placing nips along my collar bone. "You are my addiction, Ashley Hawthorne. The one thing I'm not supposed to have but can't stop thinking about." His tongue peeks out, licking the hollow between my neck and shoulder, causing my whole body to erupt into goosebumps. "If death is the price I have to pay, then so be it. This moment is worth every second of bliss."

My body arches and I release another moan into the air. His fingers have found their way to my damp panties, pushing them aside and running them along my slit in one smooth movement.

"My god, Titus. Yes." I let out a half growl half grown, needing him inside me already.

"Yes, what, *min skatt*?" His digits linger, hovering above my swollen nub, gently rubbing circles and driving me mad.

"Yes. More. Yes. I'm yours. Yes. Please." I'm spitting out incoherent fragments of words, hoping one of them is the *open sesame* to the treasure trove of pleasure he possesses in his hands.

Titus' mouth finds mine, his tongue licking the slit asking for entry, but my greedy mouth wants more. Sucking his tongue, I try and soak him in. His scent, his breath, his sounds. I want all of him, and even then, it won't be enough.

Two thick fingers find their way inside my core and I contract around them, biting his tongue as a multitude of nerves dance in ecstasy.

This is heaven on earth, this man's embrace, his undivided devotion to my body and its pleasure. I couldn't be any happier.

He begins to slowly pump his digits in and out of me, making me ride his hand with every push and pull.

"Fuck, Titus. This feels so good."

Like a record player halting to a screech, tapping on the window has me jolting back. As soon as my eyes look out the window I see the back of Hudson's Henley.

Oh my god, oh my god, oh my god.

My entire body is on fire as the heat of embarrassment washes over me.

"You two might want to move this show elsewhere, William is about to come out any minute and I doubt you'd want him finding out about you two like this." Hudson speaks toward the home and away from the car. I could not be more thankful for this courtesy right now.

"Ten-four." Titus' commanding voice is stoic, not an ounce of shame or panic to be found.

Just as easily as he plucked me from my seat, he lifts me up and carries me back over the console, squeezing my thigh in reassurance as he knocks on the window. As soon as Hudson turns around, Titus gives him a two-finger salute.

Not waiting for a second chance, I push the start button, revving the engine and getting us out of dodge.

That was insanely close. *Too close.*

I'm not ashamed of what I feel for Titus, but that's definitely not the way I'd want William to find out about us.

If there even is an *us.*

Chapter Ten

TITUS

I'm one lucky son of a bitch.

Keeping my gaze focused on the road ahead of us, I don't let Ashley see my face. No, I'm not a very emotive person. But somehow she can usually tell if something's off with me.

And right now, something's definitely off.

"So, um... that was close." She gurgles and coughs in what I think is a nervous laugh.

Okay, that definitely has me looking.

"That's a new sound." My lips tilt into a smirk, unable to hold back the playful jab.

Ashley's hand flies up to swat at me and I can't help but grasp her hand in mine, bringing it to my mouth for a nip. "Raise that hand at me again, and you won't be able to sit for a week, little treasure."

Ashley's body trembles and her face flushes. "Are you into that? Spanking?"

There's an awkward pause before I tell her a version of the truth.

"There's a lot you don't know about me, Ashley. Things I would never dream of telling you. You're too damn good for me to taint. I could never forgive myself." I scoff as I fling myself back into the headrest. "Fuck. Your brother would never forgive me."

The car screeches to a halt, sending me flying toward the dash.

"Enough with my brother! This, whatever this is," Ashley waves her hands in the air like a madwoman. "Is between you and me. If you don't think it's worth the risk–that I'm worth the risk–then it's best we clear that up right now."

"Not worth the risk? Is that why I practically fucked you in front of your brother's house?" I shake my head in disbelief. How can she possibly think that after what we just did? "It's not that you're not worth it, it's that you're worth far too much. I don't want to ruin you. You deserve a normal relationship, with a normal partner who enjoys doing all the high-society things you like to do. Me? I can't stand those things. I stick out like a sore thumb, feeling like an alien in a human suit. Trust me, princess. People don't look at you and pair you with someone like me."

Ashley snorts. She literally snorts. What the hell?

"Is that what you think of me? That I like doing all that hoity-toity shit?"

"Well, that's what you did with Brad, and what you've done with all your friends back home for as long as I can remember."

"My god. The only reason I ever go to those things is as a favor to my friends and then boyfriend. I hate those events just as much as you do." Ashley raises a finger in the air and smirks. "And for the record, if you stick out like a sore thumb, it's because you're most likely the hottest man there. No socialite's husband or boyfriend has their muscles practically ripping their suits at the seam. Have you looked in the mirror? What woman in their right mind wouldn't like a ride on the Titus Express."

Biting my cheek, I hold back a full-blown grin, "Hey, there's nothing 'express' about me."

Ashley rolls her eyes. "Don't I know it. So, do you have any more excuses as to why you don't want to be with me?"

"They aren't excuses, and I never said I didn't *want* to be with you. It's more of a can't." I let out a breath of frustration. "Look. It's for the best. You need something more than I could ever give you. I'm not the family type. I'm definitely not conventional. And my idea of a good time is definitely not mainstream. Why start something that's only going to end up in heart break?"

"Well, you sure are full of yourself. Do I need to remind you that I'm a grown woman in charge of my own actions and emotions? It's extremely arrogant of yourself to think that I'm some little damsel who'd fall at your feet like some dumbstruck fool, unable to look at a good time for what it is. Just some simple fun."

Her words hit deep. If I were being honest, I wasn't entirely referring to her feelings, but mine as well. She's got a hold on me unlike any other, and I fear that I'd lose myself in her, unable to escape.

I care for her, and I want to make her whole. Letting myself enjoy her would only achieve the opposite, wouldn't it?

"It's not that simple, Ashley. Your brother has also tasked me with looking after you. I've already betrayed him with everything we've done. To keep doing it, keep lying to him. It wouldn't be right."

Ashley rolls her eyes, "I don't need you looking after me. I'm not a helpless child. If you want to use that as an excuse for not fucking me, then that's on you. I'm not going to beg you to be with me."

My palm slams onto the dashboard, the loud thud echoing in the small cabin as Ashley's body stills. "Enough! Those are not excuses! Someone is after your family and our fooling around has already cost me precious time, I should have been dedicating to finding out who's behind it all. I will *not* risk your safety for a hot fuck, despite how much I want it. You're worth more than that. Don't you get that?"

Shaking her head, Ashley places the car in drive. "Oh, I get it. It's crystal clear. Your job is to keep me safe. You don't do emotions. And you definitely don't fool around with your friend's little sister."

Tilting my head back, I ask for patience. "You're infuriating, woman. One day you'll see this was for the best." The heels of my palms press at my eyes rubbing as I ask myself if that's even true.

With what I'm giving up, it better well damn be.

ACTS OF GRACE

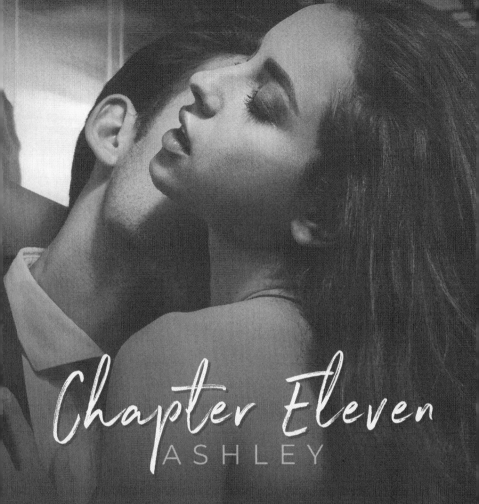

Chapter Eleven

ASHLEY

"I'm so glad we could find some girl time." Bella looks at me from over her glass of wine.

Yes, I'm aware she's only eighteen, but the woman acts as if she were older than me.

With everything she's been going through—and on top of that, caring for my niece and her twin brothers—I'm definitely not going to tell her she needs to put down that drink.

If anything, I'm liable to pour her another.

"Me too. I know I sure needed the distraction." I take a generous sip of my favorite rosé before placing the bottle back in the silver ice bucket.

Bella's brows raise up, "Do tell. It's nice to know that I'm not the only one with a hot mess life."

I look around the cabana where we've run off to for some quiet time, making sure that there aren't any prying ears. Specifically, those belonging to my brother, William.

Once I'm comfortable that it's just the two of us, I let it rip. "It's a really long story. But the gist of it is that the lawyer I was dating, Brad, is a no-good cheater. Worst part of it all is that all of our friends knew he'd been going around my back with his secretary, yet none thought it appropriate to let me know." I raise my glass, panning the pool in front of me. "Not a single damn one. I get that they were his friends first and I was the newcomer to the friendship, but still, any decent person should have said something. At the very least hinted at it. But nooooo, instead I was walking around at every function like some damn fool. The joke was on me."

One of Bella's delicate hands is covering her mouth as she gasps in horror. "My god. They're all fucking assholes."

Raising my glass to her, "Cheers to that. They can all take a hike for all I care. They're all dead to me." I bring my glass to my lips, letting the coolness soothe the sting. "But you know, part of me thinks it's my fault. I should have made more friends outside of his circle. Instead, I dedicated myself to one man, thinking that this was what I was supposed to do."

Bella lifts one finger in the air, "Nope. Stop right there. Do not second guess yourself. You thought you had friends. It's not your fault they ended up being shit heads. Any good human being would've seen that something heinous was going on and that you deserved to know."

Taking a toothpick, I stab at a grape. "It is what it is at this point. I'm just glad that things didn't go further with him. Could you imagine if I would've been saddled to that man without knowing who he really was?"

"Girl, you know the WRATH men wouldn't have let that happen. I wouldn't be surprised if they'd already had a tail on you." She raises a brow as her lips purse to the side.

"Ugh, don't even get me started on that." I groan, throwing my head back onto the lounge.

Bella chortles, "I *know* you must feel as smothered as me. William is no joke when he's on a mission. I can't go to the mailbox without having ten men watching my every move. Poor Cassie, my best friend, had to get used to my entourage every time I paid her a visit back home."

She's given me the perfect segway to ask her about my brother, and I'm not about to miss it. "So, how have you liked working and living with William? I know the live-in part wasn't something we discussed when you first interviewed for the nanny position, but I can see that Harper is extremely fond of you. Having you so close is so good for her."

My thoughts flash back to Harper's biological mother, Heather. That woman was the definition of a gold digger if I ever saw one. I think she had Harper just to snag William.

"Um, it's definitely got its ups and downs." Looking at her closely, I see she's looking off into the distance, unable to look me in the eye. "I love working with Harper. She's such a sweet baby, and the twins have grown so fond of her. They've come a long way since pouring salt in the chocolate fondue at her baptism party." She shakes her head and sighs as I practically spit out my wine.

"Oh my god! I almost forgot about that! I can't believe that was only a year ago.

Do you remember Heather's scream? I'm surprised the

neighbors didn't call the cops."

"Yes! She's such a drama queen. I wish she'd leave William alone." Bella's eyes narrow and her grip tightens around her glass.

"Bella, can I ask you something personal?"

Her eyes dart back to me nervously, "Um, sure."

I smile. Her response doesn't sound very assuring, but I really want to know.

"Is there something going on with you and William? And before you answer, know that I'm not judging, nor will I ever. I myself have always had a crush on an older man who, in a way, is off-limits."

Her dark brows reach toward her hairline. "Really!? Who?"

"Nope. I asked you first, so you have to spill the beans before I do. Those are the rules."

"W--" Bella opens her mouth to respond but is cut off by my brother's booming voice.

"Bella. Harper needs her stuffed rabbit, and I can't find it anywhere." William is talking to Bella, but his eyes are staring daggers into me.

Was this prick eavesdropping?

Oh, hell no.

"Yes, of course. Last I saw, it was in her highchair. She was trying to feed it cheerios." Her eyes light up at the memory and it makes my heart squeeze. You can see she really does care for my niece. "Men. Helpless creatures, aren't they?" She shakes her head and laughs as she gets up from her seat. "I'll be right back. Just going to rescue the Jellycat bunny."

As soon as Bella isn't within earshot, William lays into me. "What the hell were you doing?"

"What was *I* doing? Oh, brother. That's rich. If I'm not

mistaken, you were listening in on our *private* conversation. This," I wave my hands in front of him, "is going over the line. How do you think she's going to react to your overbearing ways? You're going to lose her, and it won't be because of my questions. I can assure you that."

William's eyes narrow as he steps closer, hovering over me. "I'm not being overbearing. And losing her is not my concern. She isn't mine, so therefore, I can't lose what I never had."

I stand up, needing to get from under his hovering. Standing up on my tippy toes I stab at his chest with my finger. "You forget one thing. I know you. We grew up together. You're falling head over heels for that woman and there's nothing you can do to stop it." His eyes go from narrowed to widened pools of concern. Patting him on the chest, I smile. "Don't worry, brother. She's falling for you too. But a piece of advice, come clean about our family history. You *will* lose her if you don't tell her."

William steps back as if I've scorched him with my words. "Advice? From you? Why would I take relationship advice from you? From what I heard, you couldn't even figure out your lame boyfriend of over a year had been cheating on you."

It's my turn to step back, practically stumbling back into my chair. My chest stings, not because I miss my ex, but because he's right. I was so dumb I didn't even see the betrayal happening.

"William," Titus roars. That's it, no other words follow. Turning around, I see Titus staring daggers into my brother.

William rubs at the back of his neck as he squeezes his eyes shut. "Ashley, I'm sorry. That was a dick thing to say."

My eyes flicker back and forth between my brother and Titus. *Had he been here the whole time? Was he eavesdropping too? Why did he feel the need to step in, like my knight and shining armor, scolding my brother like some sort of parent figure?*

"Ashley?" William calls to me, but I'm so upset I have nothing to say. I just stand there, brows pushed together, shaking my head.

Bella's voice calls out, breaking us from our staring match. "What's going on?"

"Ashley and I need to talk about something. Mind letting me break into your girls' night?" Titus looks to Bella, offering her the closest thing to a smile he has—a smirk.

Bella's eyes light up as she looks back and forth between Titus and me, her eyes going wide as she bites back a smile. "Of course! We can catch up later. You too have fun! There's cheese and grapes in the bar fridge in case you need more."

William ushers her out of the cabana with his hand on the small of her back. "They aren't having a date night, Bella. It's just Titus and Ashley."

My brother's words have me waking from this daze of anger. *How dare he!?* Before I know what I'm doing, my legs are carrying me forward, about to demand he take back every word. The date, the thing about my ex, my advice—all of it. He needs to take it all back.

Two strong arms wrap around my waist and hold me back. "Ashley, don't. You both need time to cool off." His words are low, whispered into the hollow of my neck.

Normally I'd welcome this closeness, but not now. Not after he's made his position with me crystal clear.

"Don't touch me!" I wiggle and kick my way out of his hold. Although, I know that he had to of let me go free, otherwise there's not a move on this earth that could pull me out of his grasp.

Whirling around, I give him a piece of my mind. "Cool off?

You want me to cool off, after what you both just did? Don't think it's escaped me that you were listening in on what was supposed to be a private conversation between Bella and me." My body is vibrating with rage, I can hardly stand still. "No. You do not get to tell me to cool off. and you definitely don't get to lay one single finger on me. Ever."

"Is that a challenge?" His eyes darken into that unmistakable shade of indigo.

"Are you deaf? No, that isn't a challenge. You men think that Bella and I are here at your disposal, your control. Well, newsflash, we're not. We're our own people and if you don't give us the respect we deserve, don't expect any of it in return. Much less any willing affection."

Titus prowls over to me, his body lingering a mere breath away. "*Min skatt*. You can't mean that." His tone is deep yet gentle, trying to tame my aching heart. "Above everything, we're friends."

I sneer at that. "No. Friend's don't eavesdrop on friends."

"I'm sorry. That was wrong of us."

My mouth opens and closes, unsure of what to say now. I was used to arguing with Brad, a man who never apologized or acknowledged any wrongdoing.

Hell, it took him cheating on me for him to finally say those two magical words, 'I'm sorry.'

Titus pulls me by the hands toward the lounge and lowers me onto his lap.

"I couldn't stop him. He was hell bent on finding out what happened to you in Florida. I hadn't delivered the information he wanted, so he thought he'd dig it up himself." Titus chuckles, his chest heaving up and down, rubbing against my arm. Involuntarily, my body leans into him, seeking his warmth.

"That still didn't give him or you the right to listen in on our conversation. That's all kinds of wrong."

His firm hand finds its way to my back, rubbing slow circles. "I know. I practically ripped his vocal cords out when he all but blamed you for your ex cheating on you." His eyes harden and his nostrils flare. "I should've stopped him sooner."

For the first time since the men's intrusion, I'm actually smiling. Titus is genuinely offended on my behalf.

"Okay, so what does he want to know?" I cock a brow and purse my lips. If I were a betting woman, I'd say Titus is dying to know as well.

"He's figured out Brad's infidelity. We have a pretty good team out there and they've been able to give him the details as to what went down, but not the why."

"Why?" I laugh. "Why does any man cheat? Boredom, insecurity, gluttony?"

Titus hands reach up to my face, cupping them with such tenderness. "No, Ashley. Why did it hurt you so much? It was apparent you didn't love Brad. He didn't think you two would last much longer, and hell, I had basically blocked him from memory. If either of you had mentioned him, it must have been so casually because the rest of the team wasn't even aware that you were dating."

I close my eyes and take in a deep breath, before releasing my truth. "I didn't want to be alone."

Shame washes over me and there's nowhere for me to hide. My body heats and my eyes tingle with the promise of tears, so I do the only thing I can think of. Shut my eyes. Hide the pain and emptiness. Keep it inside.

The pad of Titus' thumb wipes away a tear. "My little treasure. Only you would feel alone while being overrun with a security team and an overbearing brother."

My eyes fling open. What the? Here I am, laying out my feelings and all he can do is discredit them? I'm about to tear into Titus for being an insensitive jerk when I see he's smirking.

"Great. Now that you've stopped crying and I have your attention... You are not alone. You have a brother who loves you more than life, you have the team, which is like an extended family, and of course, you will always have me."

A soft smile tugs at my lips. "Thank you for trying to make me feel better, Titus, but I don't have you. I never have and I never will."

I take one last look at this gorgeous man, the sloped angles of his face begging to be kissed and commit them to memory. He was never meant to be mine, and nothing we do or wish for will make it so.

Getting up from his lap, I turn away from him, heading toward the house.

Without a glance back, I wave goodbye.

Goodbye to what was.

Goodbye to what isn't; and

Goodbye to what could be.

Chapter Twelve

TITUS

"Come on, man. It's been almost seven days since you came back to town. This is the first time you've been out, the least you could do is put on a smile." Hudson chortles before rolling in his lips. "Well, a smile by your standards is more of a smirk."

"Ha ha. I'm not amused." I survey the club scene, and even though this place isn't my norm, there should still be enough to catch my interest.

"I'm not here to amuse you. I'm here to snap you out of whatever weird mood you've been in. I swear, every time I look at you, I'm unsure if you're constipated or just depressed."

I give him the side eye. The sad part is, he's not wrong.

I can't be with her, yet nobody else can even make my dick twitch.

"What about that brunette over there." Hudson points at a petite woman with wavy brown hair by the bar.

For a second there, my heart clenches. The woman looks so much like Ashley, but of course it's not her. "No. No fucking brunettes." I snort at my unintentional pun.

"What's so funny?" Hudson's brows come together as he studies my face.

"Nothing. Just, no brunettes."

"Uh-huh. Nothing my ass." He takes a swig of his vodka tonic, his judging eyes never leaving my face. "Look, man. It's clear you're hung up on whatever you and Ashley had."

"We didn't have anything," I growl.

"Save it and hear me out." Hudson raises a hand, palm exposed. "We both know there's always been an unspoken rule about little sisters." His face puckers as if he's tasted a lemon, but doesn't elaborate. He doesn't have to, I know full well what he's saying is true.

"And?"

"That rule is the only thing holding you back from Ashley, and clearly the reason behind your constipation."

"I'm not constipated, fucktwad."

"Right. Well, anyway, like I was saying... This is clearly something more than just a fling. Something enough that could obliterate that unspoken rule and maybe give you and Ashley a real chance at something."

His words dig deep, stirring something in my black heart and making it spark to life—but then common sense hits. There's no way William would be okay with this even if my intentions with her were pure. Something I can't even convince myself of. Every time I see Ashley, all I want to do is dirty her up. Fuck her so raw that she's left nothing but a mess of tangled hair, sweat and cum. There's nothing pure about that.

Looking back to Hudson, I shake my head. "No, man. Even if what you're saying is true, I'm not what Ashley needs. She needs someone who's strait-laced. Someone who'd give her a family, the proverbial picket fence and all that shit. Not me. I wasn't made for that."

"Okay. If you say so." A blonde approaches our VIP table, sashaying past us. "Hey, doll. My friend here's been admiring your beauty all night. Couldn't take his eyes off you. Only problem is, he's a bit shy."

The tall blonde looks me over, licking her lips as her eyes take in every inch. Before I know it, she's lowered herself onto my lap, arms hooked around my neck. "Well, Daddy. I bet I can fix that."

One of her hands trails down my arm, slowly hovering over my biceps and forearms and stopping at my Patek Philippe. Of course she wouldn't miss the three-hundred-thousand-dollar watch.

I'm not a flashy man, but this is the one luxury I allow myself. It was a gift from my mother. When she escaped Europe, she didn't have much. Just this watch and me in her womb.

Pulling my hand away, my lip curls. Having enough of Hudson's experiment, I take both of her hands and stand her up. "Thanks, *doll.* I think there's been a mistake. My friend here has had one too many. I'm not looking for anyone tonight."

The blonde looks back and forth between the two of us, a mixture of confusion and frustration marring her face.

"Cindy," I call to our waitress who arrived with a fresh bottle of vodka. "Would you mind setting up our friend here with a table in the VIP? Place her charges on my tab."

At my words, the woman's demeanor transforms from sour to sweet. Good, hopefully that's enough to make up for Hudson's asshole move.

I'm all for a good mind fuck but all parties have to consent. Otherwise, it's just plain cruel and I don't do cruel. At least not with women.

As soon as Cindy and the blonde have cleared the area, Hudson pipes up. "So much for you not having a thing for Ashley. I've never seen you turn down a fun time. And that woman," his thumb points back toward the blonde, "was in for a good time."

"That woman was in for a sugar daddy. You need to be able to spot them better or you'll end up like poor William. Last I heard, Heather is wanting to drop the divorce since she found out the prenup gives her nothing if she leaves."

Hudson shakes his head, "I wouldn't wish that woman on our worst enemies."

"You say that but here you are, trying to saddle me with Heather's clone."

"Look man, I love you like a brother so I'm always going to give it to you straight. Seems to me like the only thing holding you back is you. I've seen the way that woman looks at you. You could be a raging pile of dog shit and Ashley would still look at you like you hung the moon."

"What is it with you and shit? You have some weird obsession with fecal matter we don't know about?"

Hudson rolls his eyes. "That is *not* my kink. Stop trying to change the subject. What I'm trying to say is that you're so hung up on you not being the right guy for her, when really, that's

116

something she should be deciding for herself. You can't make that call for her."

I stand, having enough of Hudson's intervention. "Thanks for the advice, brother, but you don't know what the hell you're talking about." I take one last sip from my glass before slamming it on the table. "I'll be out of pocket for the next twenty-four hours. If you need me, use the back line."

Hudson's lips roll in, fighting a smile. "Mhm. Send Ashley my regards."

Giving him my back, I head toward the valet. I'd knock his lights out if he weren't so damn right.

There's only one place I want to be right now, and it sure as fuck isn't Dallas.

Ashley

TITUS: come outside.

I blink at the screen, waiting for the text message to disappear. This can't be real right? The last time I spoke to Titus, things weren't exactly friendly.

TITUS: NOW.

My stomach flutters at the command. Could he really be here?

Quickly throwing on a soft cardigan over my silk camisole and pants, I head for the door. There's only one way to find out and I'm not waiting around in my room.

The night air smells of freshly cut grass but it's devoid of Titus' signature scent. Okay? Where is he?

TITUS: head to the left of the drive.

Okaaaay. This is getting stranger and stranger. If I weren't sure we had the home surrounded by guards, I'd be heading back in. This is something straight out of a horror movie where you're yelling at the screen telling the girl to not go in the basement.

I reach the end of the drive when a pair of strong hands I know all too well reach out and pull me behind a large oak.

"*Min skatt.*" His deep voice rumbles through me, making my legs shake.

"Titus," I whisper. "What are you doing here?"

Looking up into his eyes, I see his pained stare. "I needed to talk to you."

"Okay. I'm here. Talk."

"You know I don't do relationships. I wasn't built for it."

I cock a brow, wondering where the hell he's taking this. "Yes, and?"

He takes in a deep breath, looking up at the house before continuing. "But what I can do are agreements."

"Agreements?" My brows drop as they push together. "What kind of agreements?"

His eyes come back to me, making my chest vibrate with pent up emotion. "I've never done this before. Not with someone I know well. But if you'll accept, it would be exclusive. A physical relationship between the both of us where you're willing to try out... different things."

I bite the inside of my cheek, unsure of what to say. Is he talking about a sex contract? "But it would be exclusive right?"

His eyes light up, like a little kid at Christmas. "Yes. Just you and me."

Biting my lower lip, I smile. "Okay. I'd like to hear more about these 'different things' you'd want to try."

Titus picks me up by the waist and twirls me around. "How

about I show you?"

Carrying me bridal style, he takes me to a blacked-out SUV down the road. "What about the guards, won't they see us leaving together?"

Titus chuckles. "They know better than to say anything. The five WRATH men are equal partners. They wouldn't dare rat one of us out to the rest. Not if they know what's good for them."

Titus pulls the back-passenger door open and slides me in, quickly following and closing the door behind him.

All of a sudden, nerves that had been lying dormant show up like ants at a picnic and I start running my mouth. "Wow, the backseat. I haven't gotten it on in the backs—"

"No." Titus presses his fingers to my lips as his jaw clenches and nostrils flare. "No talk of you and anyone else. Ever. Understood?"

I nod my head slowly, kissing the pad of his fingers.

Titus purses his lips at that. "Remember our word?"

"Diamonds," I breathe out, my voice husky and low.

"Good girl." Titus sits in the middle of the back seat, grabbing me by the waist and hoisting me over him so that I'm straddling his hips while facing him. "If any of this gets too uncomfortable or you want to stop, use our word."

I nod slowly as excitement begins to wash over my nerves.

Slowly laying me down the center console, Titus grabs the right passenger seatbelt and then the driver's, bringing them both toward me and binding my arms above my head.

My breathing picks up and nipples harden. Never in my life have I done anything like this.

If I were being honest, I'd only been with a handful of men and none of them were worthy of mention.

"You okay, *min skatt*?" Titus' eyes are a mixture of concern and lust, his inner battle as apparent as my heaving chest. "Yes, Titus. I want this. I want you."

The skin around his eyes crinkles and his luscious lips form into a devilish smile. "Good, because I want you. And I'm not holding back."

ACTS OF GRACE

Chapter Thirteen
TITUS

*L*aying before me is a goddess.
Into the pits of my darkness I will drag her, marring her
creamy skin with my seed.

Pristine and precious like her name suggests, my little treasure
will be devoured whole, fulfilling my need.

Lifting up her camisole, exposing the luscious mounds of
perfection, I can't help but lower my mouth to a dusky pink nipple
and rolling the hardened bud between my teeth.

"Ahhh." Ashley moans as she arches her back into me, begging
for more.

Taking clamps out, I slowly clip them on to both hardened nubs,
making sure to give her enough time to object with our safe word.

One look into those doe eyes and I know she's all in. She's all mine. "My dirty little treasure. You're mine. Mine to cherish. Mine to play with. Mine to wreck."

A wicked little smile plays on her lips as she bites the corner of her bottom lip.

She's stunning.

My eyes can't seem to land on a single spot. Taking her all in, they finally land on the silver chain glistening in the moonlight as it ties the two small clamps together, making my cock twitch.

This is going to be

So

Damn

Good.

Giving it a little tug, Ashley moans.

"My god. I feel it down there." Her face heats, making me grin like the cat that ate the canary.

"Say it, *min skatt*. Pussy. You feel it in your *pussy.*"

Her mouth opens, a tiny pink tongue peeks out licking her upper lip. "Pussy. I feel it in my pussy."

My fucking god.

I'm lost.

It is me who is ruined.

This pure princess, talking dirty just for me. *How could any other do?*

My hands travel from her splayed arms, digging my nails into her soft flesh, dragging them down the curves of her luscious body.

Art.

That's what she is.

Reaching her hips, I squeeze, before hovering a hand over her jean clad pussy—slapping it before ripping the bottoms off in one smooth move.

"Your turn." Ashley's eager eyes rove over me and I can't help but smirk.

"It *is* my turn." Hands to my collar, I undo my tie before taking the dark blue silk to her beautiful face. "Close your eyes, baby."

Ashley's already large eyes widen even further before shutting in compliance.

"Good girl." I lower my lips to the shell of her ear, gently knotting the tie around her eyes. "If you listen to Daddy, I'll give you what you want."

Her breathing picks up and her chest quickly rises and falls to the cadence of our desire.

"Yes, Daddy."

"*Fuuuuck, baby.*"

My fingers dig into her hips as I thrust my clothed pelvis into her bare ass.

If I thought I was a goner before, I was so fucking wrong.

I almost nutted in my slacks from those words alone.

Not only is she willing to give me her body, but she's given me her mind.

Taking my thumb to her clit, I lazily rub circles, listening to her panting get louder and louder.

"Does my baby want more?"

"Mhm." She nods emphatically while pressing her lips together.

Taking my hands below her ass, I lift her up. Bringing her mound to my mouth, I lick it from base to clit before sucking in the tiny nub and flicking it with my tongue.

"Oh god. Yes!" Ashley's thighs grip my head and I chuckle into her folds.

I feel the skin around my eyes crinkle from smiling. "Baby, drop your knees."

Never have I been this gentle with a partner before. This is something new to me, but I can't find it in me to command Ashley any other way.

I already feel as if I've stolen something that should never be mine. Treating her like any other sub just feels wrong.

"Well, Daddy? Are you going to fuck me or are you going to breathe over my pussy all night."

I throw my head back and laugh, my lips lifting into an impossibly large smile. "Little brat, it's me who gives the orders. Not the other way around."

Ashley smirks, lifting her pelvis to me. "Yes, Daddy. Now lick your naughty girl's pussy. It's aching for you."

My fucking god. She really will be the death of me.

Taking three fingers at once, I thrust them into her tight entrance as my mouth comes down, licking and sucking.

In and out, I thrust, her juices running down my fingers and making my cock pulse with the need to be inside her.

Applying pressure to her walls I feel her begin to close around me, pulling my fingers in with every contraction.

"Yes, Daddy. Yessssssss." She hisses as she climbs that mountain of pleasure before free-falling into that delicious state of bliss, her moans and whimpers never stopping as her whole body becomes limp in my arms.

"My god. I could never tire of your sounds." My thumb traces up and down her wetness, reveling in the shivers I illicit every time I graze her clit. "Are you ready for me, baby?"

She mewls, "Yes. More. I want more."

"Yes, what, baby girl." My eyes narrow, focusing on her plump lips.

"Yes. Daddy." The plump pillows of perfection curl up into a sinful smile, propelling me into action.

With one hand I undo my belt and unzip my slacks, finally pulling my aching dick out of its confinement.

My calloused fingers wrap around the thick girth and groan at the pressure it relieves as a tiny bead of pre-cum pearls at the head.

Taking my thumb I swipe, bringing the milky bead to Ashley's parted mouth.

"Suck." I thrust my thumb into her wet mouth and growl as she takes me, moaning in pleasure as she licks and rolls me in her mouth.

"God, you suck so good, baby."

Pulling her hips to me, I nestle my cock between her silky slit, thrusting it up and down, coating my length with her juices.

"Oh, yes. Please, put it in, Daddy."

My chest clenches, dick jumps, and breathing stops.

She's so fucking perfect.

In one swift move, I slide inside her. Stopping once I'm sucked in to the hilt.

Her tight walls swallow me, bringing me home. This is where I want to be. This is where I could live and die.

Slowly thrusting in and out, I enjoy each moan, each mewl. They're all for me. Each little sound of pleasure, she's giving it to me.

My hands anchor into her hips, fingers digging into her supple skin as I bring her to me only to pull her away.

The sounds of wet skin, slapping and sliding mixed with our ragged breathing is enough to make me want to spill my seed in her.

Sliding a hand up to her neck, I squeeze. Claiming what's

mine, what no other man will have.

"Fuck, baby. The thought of coming inside you..." My dick pulses against her walls, causing her mouth to go slack and moan. "Having you take my seed. Make you mine."

My thrusts speed up, becoming frantic as I squeeze her neck tighter—all while pushing and pulling on her delicious hips and making her ass bounce faster and faster.

"Yes, please. Fuck me faster, Daddy. Make me yours. I need to be yours."

Jesus. Christ.

I have seen heaven and it is inside of this woman.

A kaleidoscope of colors explodes before me as I release into her warm and wet pussy, never stopping my pumping. "Come with me, baby."

Her tightening walls confirm what I already know.

"Already..." she pants, "there."

My hands never leave her as we both ride out this wave of pleasure, never wanting it to end. This is quite possibly the best night of my life.

Never have I experienced whatever it is that just happened.

As I continue to pulse my release into her, I know I'm in trouble.

There's no way I could ever let *this* go.

There's no way I could ever let *her* go.

Ashley

His hands rub up and down the angry red marks on my arms.

"Shit, baby. I'm sorry." His chest rumbles with his apology.

"Don't. Don't apologize for something I wanted." I cock a brow, daring him to defy me.

"Yes. You may have wanted sex, but you didn't know it would leave you scarred." His eyes narrow as I scoff.

"Titus, these are hardly scars." My hand caresses his strong jawline before resting on the dip in his neck, my thumb tracing the outline of a faded scar. "This. This is a scar." My body shudders at the thought of what could've caused the jagged line so close to his jugular.

His strong arms wrap around me, pulling me to his chest, his lips landing on my temple with a soft kiss. "What's wrong?"

"How can you tell something's wrong?" My voice sounds small, as if I've lost myself to fear.

"Your body is trembling, *min skatt*. Talk to me. Was this too much?"

Pushing myself off of his chest a little, I look into his indigo eyes. "God, no. This was perfect." My eyes bounce back and forth between his. "No, it's the scar on your neck. It's Aiden in a coma. It's the idea that I could lose you." I suck in a breath, realizing what I've just said. "I mean, not that I have you."

I begin to crawl off of him, but he stops me, both arms pulling me back to him.

"Look at me, Ashley."

I still at his command but my eyes remain on the window.

His hands reach up, cupping my face and pulling it toward his.

"Ashley." Once my eyes are on his, he gives me three little words that shake me to my core. "I am yours."

My mouth hangs open, but nothing comes out. I doubt he's ever uttered that to anyone before. This man is a fortress of strength and stoicism. He does not do emotions. For him to tell me he is mine... I'm at a loss.

"Close that mouth of yours before you catch flies." He lifts a brow but smirks.

Taking out one of his soft kerchiefs, he cleans me up before doing the same to himself.

Thoughts of him with another woman flash before me and my stomach lurches. We didn't use protection and it's not the thought of pregnancy that scares me but what else could happen with unprotected sex. "Have you..."

His eyes meet mine, smirk still visible. "Have I what?"

"Have you been with anyone since we were last together?"

"Jesus, Ashley." His face sours, brows dropping as a pained expression takes over. He quickly puts himself away and tosses the soiled kerchief to the front passenger seat before cupping my face in his hands. "No. I would never put you in danger like that." His eyes search mine for understanding.

I slowly nod, pursing my lips to the side. "Well, neither have I...and I'm still on birth control." I quickly tack on that last bit, even though he's never asked. Something that surprises me because he's the one to always tout control.

At my words, Titus' jaw tightens and his eyes narrow—something wild flashing behind his beautiful orbs as they sear me with their intensity. "I don't care what you've done before this moment, but from now on, you are mine. These lips are mine." His fingertips caress my mouth before slowly moving to my mound, cupping it with one hand. "And this pussy is mine. Understand?"

I give him a cheeky smile and wink. "Yes, Daddy."

He throws his head back, exposing the vein along his neck as he roars in laughter. One of these days I'm going to trace that line with my tongue.

"I'll take that as you liking what we did tonight." His eyes light up in a way I've never seen before and it warms my heart. I did that. I brought him that joy.

"Yes." My cheeks hurt from how hard I'm smiling, and I don't give a damn if I look like a loon. "I loved it."

He picks up my discarded jeans and panties, repositioning me so that I can put them back on.

"Good, little treasure. That makes me happy." Placing his lips to my temple, he gives me a soft kiss. "Now, let's get you back to the house before anyone notices you're missing."

His words bring me back down to earth. I'm still his secret. This is still purely physical. He told me as much, and I agreed.

I agreed.

Chapter Fourteen

ASHLEY

*S*hit. Damn. Fuck.

William's car is parked in the drive. There's no way I can make it inside without him seeing me.

My only prayer is that he's in his bedroom or in the game room with the boys and Harper.

As soon as I push the door open, I hear a heated conversation between Bella and my brother.

So much for slipping in unnoticed. Feeling like a guilty teenager who's been caught past curfew, I try to slide by.

That's when Bella's big grey eyes land on me, taking in my disheveled hair and crumpled cami.

Giving them an awkward wave, I announce myself. "Hey, guys. What are you doing up so late?" Smooth move, Ashley. That only points out the fact that *I* was just outside so late.

William looks annoyed and doesn't even spare me a glance. "We were talking about Dad."

"So you finally told her about our cheating father?" I blink rapidly, surprised that he actually took my advice and came clean.

Bella's face pales and her face whips over to William. "Your father was a cheater?" Her nose scrunches up and her eyes narrow.

"I mean..." I try to interject, but William shoots me a death glare. Got it. That's my cue to exit. "It's late. I should probably go to bed. Taking a monitor into the room with me in case the kids need anything. You two clearly need to have a talk."

William scowls in disapproval. "We *were* having a talk before you came home. And don't think you're off the hook regarding your whereabouts tonight. We'll be talking later."

No, we won't, brother. Not unless you want to end up on America's Most Wanted *after offing one of your best friends.*

As I make my way back to my room, I can't help but think that maybe it's a good idea Titus and I agreed to a no strings attached fling.

Plopping down on my oversized king bed, I look at the evidence before me. Do happily ever afters even exist?

William is going through a divorce with a psycho, he and Bella are clearly heading down the path of a messy relationship, I've never had a successful emotional entanglement, and our parents... God, there aren't enough minutes in the day for me to count all the things wrong with their relationship.

I groan into my hands as I roll onto my stomach.

"Ash? You okay?" William's voice freaks me out, pulling me out of my self-pity.

I guess I must've left the door open. Note to self, don't throw pity parties with the door wide open.

Looking up, I see he's flustered. "Am I okay? I should be asking you that. You look like you've been through the ringer."

He runs a hand through his hair, tugging at the ends. His tell-tell sign that things are not okay.

"The hospital called about Aiden. They want Bella to come in, so I'm going to take her. I was going to ask–"

"Don't worry about the kids. I've got the monitors on and I'll be here as long as you need me."

"Thanks, Ash. I really appreciate it. I know Bella does too. The guards are posted outside and we've got the perimeter hooked up, but call us if anything out of the norm happens. I saw Heather today and she looked like she had gone off the deep end."

"Oh my god!" My hand flies up to my mouth. "Yes, of course. I'll keep an eye out and let you know if anything happens. Drive safe and keep me posted on Aiden."

William gives me a curt nod before closing the door behind him.

Rolling onto my back once more, I stare at the ceiling.

Life is a funny thing. Within the past hour I've felt annoyance, bliss, embarrassment, and now deep concern.

Everything that we know of to be true can change in the blink of an eye. Poof, gone and changed forever.

Even if all I have with Titus are stolen moments, captured in between life's chaos and upheaval, I'll cherish them with all I hold dear. Because if life has taught me anything, it's that nothing is constant and happiness never lasts.

I'm wrapping my wet hair in a towel when I hear a knock at the bedroom door. That's odd, could it be one of the guards? Peeking out of the bathroom door, I check the monitors I left on the bedside table.

Huh. The kids are all asleep in their beds.

Quickly throwing on a robe, I head out of the steamy bathroom and straight for the nine millimeter in my closet.

Once I make sure the gun is loaded, I point and aim at the door.

"It's open."

The wood door creaks open before a broad frame steps into the dimly lit room.

My chest tightens and my thighs squeeze at the memory of this man assaulting my pussy not two hours ago.

"Titus? What are you doing here?" I lower the gun, dropping it to my side as I walk it over back to the closet.

I'm up on my toes, shutting the door to the safe when I feel strong hands wrap around my waist, sliding underneath my robe and working their way up to my bare breast, cupping them before squeezing the tender nipples.

"William called. Said he needed help keeping an eye on you. So here I am. Keeping an eye on you." His breath tickles my neck and my entire body feels as if it's on fire.

"I'd say you're doing a whole lot more than keeping an eye on me." My words come out ragged, unable to catch my breath with him so close.

"I can't help it. Seeing you with a gun, ready to take care of yourself and everyone in this home. The fire in your eyes. I don't think I've ever seen a more beautiful sight." He turns me around, whisking me off my feet and carrying me over to the bed before sliding in behind me.

"What about my brother? What if they come home and see you?" I turn to face him, my hand reaching up to touch the stubble along his jawline.

"I'll figure it out. I don't want you and the kids alone while his psycho ex is out there plotting revenge."

"You know we have WRATH men watching over this house, not to mention our tricked-out security system." I grin, knowing that this isn't news to him and if he's here in my bed it's because he really must feel something more.

His eyes narrow, catching on to my teasing. "You're safer with me."

He presses me to his chest, his lips landing on the top of my head, placing a soft kiss. "Now go to bed. We don't know what's going on with Aiden and there's a good chance you'll be on kid duty tomorrow."

Titus slowly runs his fingers up my arms and I flinch. "Ahh."

"Damn it." His growl stirs things in me even though I know he's really upset. "I'm sorry, little treasure. I should've been gentler with you."

My mind goes back to the blacked-out car where my arms were restrained by seat belts and I smile. "Don't apologize for something I thoroughly enjoyed." Nuzzling my face into his chest, I ask him something that's been weighing on me ever since our last rendezvous. "Have you always done it like that, or was there ever a point in your life where your sex was vanilla?"

He chuckles, his chest bouncing up and down, making my

face ride up and down with it. "Vanilla. Oh, *min skatt*. What we did tonight, or on the jet, that was as vanilla as I've ever been."

I bury my face deep into his chest, feeling embarrassed for even asking. He must think I'm such a prude compared to the other women he's been with. I normally don't care what men think of me, but this is Titus. No matter how strong I think I am, he will always find the kink in my armor.

"Hey," Titus places his fingers under my chin, lifting my face to his. "Don't get it twisted, little one. It was still the best sex of my life."

His eyes bounce back and forth between mine, trying to convey the truth in his words, meanwhile I still hold an inkling of doubt.

"But why? It isn't even what you like."

"Turns out, it's what I love." His eyes narrow, darkening into that deep shade of blue I love so much. "Bondage has always been about control for me. Boundaries. Let's just say that my childhood wasn't the best. Trust was non-existent, and growing up, sex was just a form of release. Safe within the confines of my rules." He blows out a breath, rolling onto his back while keeping an arm under me. "But then I started high school and met your brother and the rest of the WRATH men. That was the first time I trusted anyone. They showed me that not everyone was full of selfish desires. They showed me that a true brotherhood could exist. We were there for each other, no matter what." He flings his free arm over his eyes and stills.

"This is why you find it so hard to be with me, isn't it? You see it as a betrayal." It's a statement, not a question. It's clear he sees being with me as stabbing my brother in the back.

Rolling back over to me, he hugs me to him, his forehead

touching mine. "Get some rest, little treasure. Tomorrow's going to be a big day."

Well, that was a shut down if I ever saw one. I sigh, pursing my lips to the side. "Goodnight, big Daddy."

He chuckles before kissing my forehead. "Goodnight, my treasure."

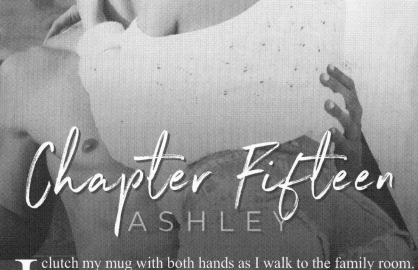

Chapter Fifteen
ASHLEY

I clutch my mug with both hands as I walk to the family room. It's been one hell of a week and with it being the day of the twins' birthday party, I need all the caffeine I can get.

When Titus said I'd be on kid duty, he wasn't kidding.

Aiden woke up from his coma, which you think would be great news, but it turns out he's basically a vegetable. We've been praying and waiting for him to come out of his current condition, where he can either remain in a persistive vegitative state or move on to talking and having actual cognitive functions.

Needless to say, Bella was a mess.

I've been watching over the twins and Harper twenty-four-seven, leaving me feeling like a windup toy at the end of its pull. Taking in another long sip of coffee, I ask myself how in the hell Bella pulls this off on a regular basis. I love my niece and the twins are a ton of fun, but holy hell. Let's just say I'm glad Bella is back in charge for today's festivities.

"Agh," I choke on the hot liquid when I catch an eyeful of William thrusting his hips into Bella's ass. Quickly turning on my heels, I wave a hand in the air. "My bad, didn't know y'all were busy with that." I'm about to walk back to my room when I hear my brother call out.

"It's okay, Ashley. You can turn around now. There's nothing to see. I was just helping Bella with the finishing touches for the party, but now that you're here..." he grins maniacally, "You can help."

Bella chimes in, wiggling her fingers as she walks out of the room. "Actually, both of you can help. I'm going to shower before the kids wake up and I need to get them ready for the day."

As soon as she's cleared the threshold, I turn toward my brother. "What the hell was that?!" I whisper-shout. "You know her father and Ren would've murdered you if they were the ones to have walked in on you like that." A pang of guilt hits me knowing he would kill Titus if he knew what we'd been up to.

I try and justify that our situation is different. Titus and I are just physical. We know our relationship won't move past that, so there's no need to inform everyone else of our agreement.

William and Bella are different. This past week they've grown closer, falling deeper down the rabbit hole of love. If they want a real relationship, he needs to come clean. Not only with her, but his best friends.

"Settle down, Ashley. I'm going to talk to them about it

eventually. I'm just waiting for the right time."

My mouth goes slack, and the feelings of guilt are overtaken by stabbing jealousy. William is willing to risk everything to be with Bella. His feelings for her are so great that he's willing to put himself out there with his best friends and business partners.

Before I know what's happening, my big green monster takes over my lips. "Oh yea? And how do you think it will go when you tell someone who's still recovering from a brain injury, or another specific someone who is extremely overprotective of their niece? I can't imagine it will go well, can you?"

"I get it, Ashley. It's a delicate situation and I promise I'll handle it with kid gloves."

"Kid gloves." I snort, unable to hold back laughter at the unintentional pun. "How fitting."

"Quit talking and help me set up this damn table." William motions to the table he and Bella were working on when I walked in.

"Okay. But hey, just so you know..." I look at him, hoping I can convey how sincere I am. "I really like Bella. She's a good woman, and even though she's only eighteen, I think she'd make an amazing partner."

William smiles, and I know he can see I really mean what I've said. "Thank you. I think so too. Now let's get to work. This isn't going to set itself up."

"Yes, sir." I giggle, remembering Titus and I the other day.

I can only hope that if our physical relationship develops into something more, my brother would be accepting of him too.

Here we go again.

I hadn't seen Titus since Aiden first woke up. I was busy with the kids and he'd flown back to Dallas for work.

But here we are, in the same damn room and he won't even look at me.

Dejavú vibes from the jet make my stomach roll.

Here I was, not two hours ago, hoping that maybe our relationship could move past something physical. That he would feel for me even a tenth of what William feels for Bella.

I shake my head. *Foolish girl.*

Heading to the kitchen, I bump into Bella who's carrying a tray of cupcakes.

"Oh my god!" I help her balance the thing, avoiding a frosting disaster. "I'm so sorry. I don't know where my head is at."

Bella's eyes light up and her lips purse to the side. "I think I have an idea." Her gaze falls behind me and I know who she's looking at.

Covering my face with both hands a grumble. "God, am I that obvious?"

"No." Bella places a hand on my shoulder as I hear the clanking of the cupcake tray rest on the marble countertop. "I know because I've been around you both for a while. Observing. Ugh, gosh. Not in a creepy stalker way. More like in a curious way. Agh. Not that you're like a sideshow experiment or anything. More like... umm, forget it."

I look at her flustered face and laugh a full bellied laugh. She always goes on rants when she's nervous. "Don't worry. I get what you're saying. I tipped you off on our girls' night that was so rudely interrupted. We need to resume that by the way. Maybe we can turn it into a weekly thing."

"I would love that. Oh before I forget, there's someone I want to introduce you to." Bella grabs my hand walking me over to a handsome man standing by the door, talking animatedly to two little girls. "Ashley, this is Jackson. He's our neighbor and father to Lilith and Lauren." The twin girls beam up at me, their eyes blinking rapidly.

"Wow, you're so pretty. Wanna come over to our house and play dolls with us? You can have Elsie."

The man chuckles, "Wow, you must be very special, Ashley. They don't even let me play with Elsie."

"I'd be honored." I look down at the girls, my cheeks hurting from how hard they have me smiling.

"Yaaay!" They cheer as they high-five each other before giving one another mischievous smiles. "Maybe you can stay for dinner and a sleepover too!"

A deep voice rumbles from behind me. "There will be no sleepovers."

Titus steps forward, his hands balled up into fists as he stares daggers into Jackson. "I'm sorry to inform you that miss Ashley can't do sleepovers."

My jaw drops at his audacity. It wasn't even Jackson who asked for the sleepover, yet Titus is over here looking at him as if he's the one who's tried to lure me away.

"Please excuse him. He has no manners." I smile at Jackson before lowering myself to the girls. "Thank you for the invite, I would love to come over and play dolls but I'm afraid I'm needed here during the night."

Bella hops in, trying to diffuse the tension. "Yes, sometimes I need to go see my dad and miss Ashley helps me by watching Matt, Max, and Harper. Speaking of, have you seen them yet? They're out back in the bouncy house."

The two blonde girls jump up and down as they screech,

"Bouncy house! Can we go, daddy?"

Jackson nods, "Of course. Be sure to take your shoes off before you go inside!" He's yelling after them as they run toward the French doors that lead to the back yard.

Bella looks between Titus and me, smirking as she heads to pick up the tray of cupcakes she'd put down earlier. "Right, well it looks like the two of you have some talking to do." She snickers as she steps between us and through to the hallway, leaving us alone in the kitchen

My eyes quickly find Titus' stoic face. Not one shred of emotion to be found after his outburst minutes ago.

"So are you going to explain what just happened?" I cock a brow, placing a hand on my hip.

"I don't know what you're talking about." His tone matches his facial cues, aloof and uninterested.

"Are you kidding me? You've been ignoring me this whole time. You didn't even greet me when you got in." I lower my voice and look at our surroundings. "You haven't even texted me all week. Then when I'm talking to the neighbor and his daughters, you come in like some sort of caveman, beating your chest and controlling my schedule." I lower the pitch of my voice, imitating his, "'There will be no sleepovers.' What the hell was that all about?"

"You won't be sleeping over any man's house. That's what that was about." His tone is steady, never wavering from the cool aloofness his face portrays. But his eyes. His eyes hold a silent fury, waiting to unleash with the write push. The right word. The right provocation.

"Jesus, Titus. It wasn't even him inviting me. It was the girls."

"It doesn't matter. I saw the way he was looking at you." The fire burning in his eyes turns molten, his body pressing closer to mine until I'm up against the wall. "You're mine, Ashley. Don't forget that."

My heart is beating rapidly, feeling as if it were going to beat right out of my chest. This is the closest we've been since he left my bed six days ago.

I may be angry with him, but my body can't help but react to his. It wants him. It craves him.

Thank god, I still have my brain because my stupid heart would acquiesce without question.

"Yours?" I scoff. "You sure have a funny way of showing it." I'm about to walk away when his arms lift to my sides, caging me in.

His tongue peeks out, licking the shell of my ear before whispering his threat, "You're mine just as I am yours. If I ever catch you entertaining the idea of a sleepover with a man, I will spank your ass so raw you won't be able to walk for a week."

My mouth opens but I have no words. I'm left gasping for air as he pins me with his heated gaze before he turns and walks out of the room.

With my back to the wall, I let myself slide down.

What have I gotten myself into?

There's no kidding myself. I'm his. But if he's to be believed, he's also mine.

Closing my eyes, I take in a deep breath.

Words, they are just words. I can't let myself fall for a man whose words are at opposites with his actions.

His faux love will not be my demise.

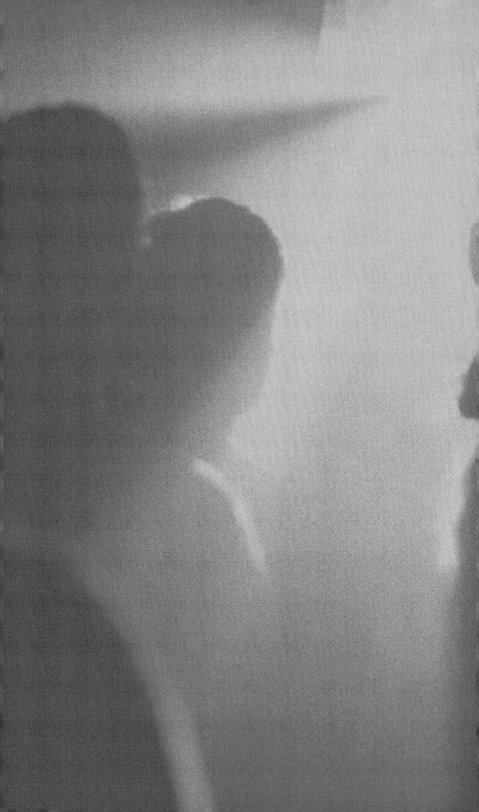

Chapter Sixteen
TITUS

What a clusterfuck of a day.

I spent the entire time at the party trying to stay away from Ashley. Every time I'm near her, all I want to do is pull her into a corner and take her.

I'm not psychic but I'm pretty sure that would end in her brother and me coming to blows.

To make matters worse, the opportunist neighbor was trying to use his girls to make a move on what's mine.

That shit won't fly.

"Grumpy much?" Hudson teases as he takes a sip of his drink.

I take a sip of Scotch, ignoring my friend's teasing and let the

We're at a bar in Malibu where a sea of tanned blondes abound—very much Hudson's choice of lay.

Looking back at my friend, I finally give him my retort. "This is what I always look like. You on the other hand, I'm surprised you're not out there picking out your beach bunnies for the night." I raise a brow, noting that he isn't being himself either.

"Didn't you get the memo?" Ren chuckles as he walks back from escorting Ashley to the lady's room. "He's into redheads now."

Hudson punches Ren in the arm, sending my brows shooting upward. "Wow, what's that about?"

Hudson narrows his eyes at Ren, "Nothing. Ren's just being a dumb ass."

Ashley smirks, "There's nothing wrong with liking redheads, Hudson."

I smile into my glass, loving the way my little spitfire had to get in on the teasing.

I let my eyes linger on her beautiful frame. She's absolutely stunning tonight. Her long hair cascades around her shoulders, showing off her ample breasts, breasts that make my mouth water remembering how delicious they taste. Following the line of her cleavage, the little black dress she's wearing hugs her tiny waist, a waist I'm dying to dig my fingers into once more.

Ren clears his throat, making me look toward him. His raised eyebrow questions me from afar, no doubt wondering what the hell I was doing eye fucking William's little sister.

What can I say? Knowing William and Bella decided to hang back at their house has me relaxing a little more around Ashley.

So what if I've given myself a little more liberty.

Raising both shoulders I smirk, as if to say, 'what are you going to do about it.'

As expected, Ren chuckles and shakes his head. He won't call me out. He knows that this would be something between me and William.

"Did someone say redheads?" The man who fell off the radar last week appears as if summoned.

Brad, Ashley's ex is at our table, staring at my woman as if he has the right.

"So this is where you've been," I growl while standing. I'm a good four inches taller than his five-eleven and I use every bit of my height to intimidate the cowardly fuck.

His green beady eyes peer up at me behind his gold rimmed frames. What did Ashley see in the dick? "Ah, I wasn't aware that you were looking for me." His face turns back toward Ashley, "Had you needed me, darling, you should have called." He tries to reach his pale hand over to Ashley's, but I intercept.

"Don't. Don't you dare fucking touch her."

Ren and Hudson stand but don't come any closer. They've got my back and will act if I need them to, but I've got this one handled.

"I'm not sure what you think you're doing here, but if Ashley wanted you, she would've called. If her ignoring the hundreds of messages you've sent her didn't give you a hint, let me do you the honors." My hand lands on his frail shoulder, squeezing with enough force that his face winces. "I'll escort you to the door where you can find your way back to the airport. You aren't wanted here."

He tries to turn around, but I've got a good grip. Despite my threats, he manages to tilt his head back and shout, "I'll call you later my love. There's so much we need to catch up about. Especially your mother!" At his words, my body tenses.

What does this fucker know about Ashley's mother?

It was my understanding that the men of WRATH were the only ones who knew about her.

Tilting my head back, I confirm that Ashley was out of earshot when this dickwad yelled out. Once I'm assured Ashley didn't hear, I motion for Hudson to follow me out. We're going to need more information from this twat before we send his ass back to Florida.

As soon as we're outside, I slam his body against the brick exterior of the building.

"Talk." I push my elbow into his chest until he squeaks.

"I—I don't' know what you're talking about." The coward has the balls to act as if he didn't just drop a bomb on Ashley."

"He's talking about Ashley's mom, you scumbag. Look, Titus is a master when it comes to torture. You don't want to get on his bad side, so I suggest you get to talking before he starts sticking keys under your nail beds." Hudson, chuckles as Brad grimaces.

The thing is, Hudson isn't exaggerating. I've actually done that before.

Pushing on Brad's chest a bit more, he starts to talk. "Okay, okay. Ashley's mom has been looking for her. That's all. She showed up in Florida and asked if I'd seen her. I know how lonely Ashley's felt, so I wanted to surprise her with the news. Maybe even win her back."

His words knock the wind right out of me.

My little treasure has been so lost, so alone, and here I've been building a wall between us, only further adding to her solitude.

"Okay, even if what you're saying is true, you know we have a tail on you. You do something, we'll be watching. You say something, we'll be listening. Tread lightly. You don't want to end up further down our shit list than you already are." Hudson begins to turn around thinking that I'm done with this fool and Brad's shoulders even drop, thinking all danger has been averted.

They're both wrong. Oh so very wrong.

I rear my hand back and punch the cheating asshole straight in the nose, blood gushing out almost immediately.

He bowls over, clutching at his face and crying out in pain. "What the fuck!? I told you what you wanted to know!"

"Yes, you did. But that didn't change the fact that you cheated on Ashley. You mess with her, you mess with me." I spit at his cowering body before wiggling my fingers goodbye. "Remember. Tread lightly."

We're headed back to the VIP area when I hear Hudson behind me, "Oh, shit!"

Turning to him I see he's pointing at where we left Ashley and Ren.

Ashley's eyes are wide open in horror as she looks at Ren talk animatedly on the phone. Her hands are up as if she wants to touch him to calm him down, but is afraid to do so.

What the hell? What could've happened since we stepped outside?

Rushing toward the two, I reach Ashley first. Pulling her into me, she shakes her head, her eyes so full of sadness.

"She's a fucking teenager, William. Have you lost your goddam mind? For fuck's sake, her father is in the hospital right now. How could you take advantage of her right now?"

My eyes widen in horror, right along with Ashley's.

William and Bella?

Bella and William?

Ren's face is beet red as he clutches the phone, pressing it tightly to his ear, "You're just lucky I'm not in front of you right now. Your mouth wouldn't be able to spew out the bullshit it's spewing because I'd be beating it in. You're batshit crazy if you think you love her... How, William? How can you love her? She's still a fucking child!"

My stomach drops and the wind is knocked out of me for a second time tonight.

Fuck. William has just confessed to loving Bella. Bella is just as off-limits as Ashley is.

You don't fuck your friends' little sisters, nieces, or daughters. You just don't.

And to fall in love... My eyes wander back to Ashley, who's undoubtedly going through the same emotions as I am.

Guilt. Horrible gut-wrenching guilt.

Ren's voice fades as I try and find a way to make this right. Fix the relationships that I've destroyed with my selfish needs.

Looking back at Hudson, he just shakes his head, as if he too is disappointed.

Fuck. What have I done?

"It *is* wrong, William. She's eighteen. One year younger and it would be punishable by law..."

I cringe, thinking Ashley isn't that much older than Bella. *Am I a cradle robber on top of everything else, too?*

Ren hurls his phone at the ground, the thing smashing into a million pieces. "Can you believe that fucking shit!?" His eyes are wild as he looks at the rest of us. "I mean, I thought we all knew family was off-limits!"

Ashley and I remain quiet, unable to muster a word, because, how could we? We're guilty of the same damn thing.

Thankfully, Hudson takes pity and decides to step in. "Is it the age thing or the family thing? You know, Bella acts much older than she is. She's been through a lot in her life and she's not your typical teenager."

Ren runs his hands through his hair, pulling at the ends. "I know man, but she's my sprout. I held her in my arms when she was born. It just doesn't feel right."

Hudson's lips roll in as he looks between Ashley and me, "Mmmmhm. You know, the way I see it, wouldn't you rather her be with someone you trust and love? There are so many ass holes out there, at least you know that if William says he loves her, he really means it. He'd never hurt her... not intentionally, at least." His shoulders rise and fall as if it's no big deal when we all know it really is.

"Don't tell me you're taking his side. Not you." Ren turns back to Ashley and me, "And you two? Are you guys on William's side too?"

Ashley and I stare at each other, not knowing what to say. To deny that Bella and William could work would be to deny us and whatever we have.

"Fuck!" Ren roars, throwing down a couple of hundred dollar bills onto the table. "I'm out of here. I can't with you guys. You two have Ashley covered. I'll see you tomorrow."

Without another word, Ren storms out of the VIP area and out into the night.

I can't say that I blame him.

William broke one of our cardinal rules.

A rule punishable by banishment from WRATH securities and worse, our friendship.

Throwing back my drink, I can't help but wince.

I'm guilty of the same crime and it's only a matter of time before I'm caught. The question is, what the hell am I going to do about it until then?

ACTS OF GRACE

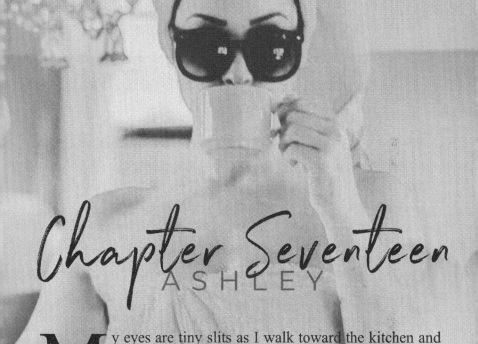

Chapter Seventeen
ASHLEY

My eyes are tiny slits as I walk toward the kitchen and my only savior...

St. Coffee.

The guys and I stayed at the bar, drinking the night away.

Ren storming out was a definitive moment in whatever relationship I had with Titus—*Yes, I'm using past tense because after the show Ren and William put on last night, I highly doubt he'll want to continue our agreement.*—Anyway, we all knew it was nothing but shitty days ahead for a while, so we drank.

We drank to forget. We drank to ease the discomfort. We drank to feel a semblance of bliss amidst the tragedy–a definite end to an era.

And now I'm suffering. I feel like a vampire, shrugging away from the light, not wanting its lethal rays of death to pierce my hungover brain.

"Ashley?" Bella's tiny voice has me fully peeling both eyes open, practically hissing at the windows.

"Hey." My voice is rough as if I'd just chain smoked an entire pack of cigarettes. "How are you?"

I'm definitely worried about how she's holding up after Ren chewed William out.

"Me?" Bella squeaks. "You look like you just got mowed down by a Mardi Gras float. All you're missing is the beads."

I snort, pulling up my knotted hair into a messy but. "Good one. I'll have to remember that." Pulling out a mug from the cabinet, I turn to look her in the eye. "I'll talk if you talk. I think we both had equally shitty nights, only I wasn't on kid duty so glug glug for me." I raise the empty mug to my mouth and mimic throwing back cocktails.

Bella bowls over with laughter, clutching onto her stomach. "Oh my god. Glug glug? Are you still drunk?"

Placing my mug under the espresso maker, I fiddle with the buttons trying to make the damn thing work. "No. I'm just at a point in my life where I could care less about being prim and proper all the time. Sometimes I just don't give a fuck and I want to be able to act like it. You know?"

Bella looks at me, jaw practically hitting the floor. Stalking toward me she inspects me closer. "Yes, it's still Ashley Hawthorne I'm talking to." She shakes her head as she grabs a mug for herself. That's when I see her swollen eyes. She'd been doing some suffering of her own last night. "I'll go first since I was supposed to go last time."

I smile at how sweet she is. She definitely doesn't have to go first, it's not like I'd hold her to it. *But that doesn't mean I'm going to stop her. I'm no fool.* Following her to the breakfast nook, I sit on the bench across from her. "I don't really know where to start, so I'll just come out and say it. William and I are together." She says that last bit really fast while wincing as if I were to hit her for it.

"Bella, seriously. I would never be mad at you for that. I'm not like the men of WRATH. So opposed to family and friends dating." I roll my eyes as I take a sip of the rich black liquid, the bitterness serving as a much needed wake up call.

Bella sighs, blowing on her drink before looking up at me with her big gunmetal eyes. "Thank god. I don't know how I'd take it if you were upset with me too."

"Look, I know Ren. Not for as long as you have—obviously, because he's your uncle—but I know him well enough. He will come around. He may seem like he's a million miles away right now, but the big goon loves you both so much. There's no way he'd stay away for long." I reach forward, cupping her hands in mine. "Once he sees that you two are serious and that you're staying together no matter what, he will have no choice but to come around. There's no way he could stay away."

Bella finally chuckles, blowing a loose strand from her face. "But what if when he finally comes around, he gets into a fight with William? I can't stand the idea of either of them getting hurt."

"That's something they will have to figure out between themselves. But you're worth it, and I know my brother thinks so too."

Bella shoots me a megawatt smile. "You really think so? I mean, I know what he tells me but it's always good to have a woman's perspective."

"Yes, that man is a goner for you." I raise a brow and smirk. "And you're a goner for him. I really am happy for the both of you. I'm also jealous that you have that type of love from a man. A man who's willing to stand up for your love. Values what you two hold and isn't willing to give it up. Not even for his business or friendships." My hand slams onto the table, the loud smack of flesh on wood reverberating through the room.

Someone clears their throat to my right. Still dealing with my hangover, I'm not sure if what I'm seeing is a mirage or if it's real.

Titus in a tight grey Henley, black jeans and black leather steel-toe boots. "Ladies." He greets the both of us, but has me pinned with his stare.

"Gentleman," I respond at the same time as Bella squeaks.

I think this whole Ren situation has her anxiety on high because she's not usually this skittish.

"I'm here to check on William." Titus' gaze remains on me even though the statement was directed toward Bella.

Bella breaks into our staring match, "I'll go get him. He's in the sh—I mean, sleeping."

That gets Titus attention. "You don't have to sugar coat shit around me, Sprout. I'm *happy* for you and William, a man who's willing to stand up for your love." Titus' words are forced, but not because he doesn't mean them, but because they are mine.

It's what I'd just told Bella I was jealous of.

Well, too bad. I'm not taking them back. It is what it is, and I feel what I feel.

Bella smirks, looking between the two of us. "Right, well he's in the shower then. I'll go tell him you're here." She gets up mumbling to herself, something about how good it is to act normal around friends.

I laugh, burying my face into my hands, barely holding back my delirium. "She's right."

Titus' brows furrow as he looks at me—a hot mess still in last night's makeup, baggy shirt hanging off one shoulder and a pair of men's boxers rolled up at the waist. "What's so funny?"

"Oh, the fact that she and William just went through what we feared and they're still standing. In fact, she even gets to act normal around friends." I motion between him and me. "We're the friends in case you missed it."

"No, I didn't miss it." His eyes darken as soon as they land on my waist. "Whose are those? You didn't have anyone stay the night, did you?"

My jaw drops at his blatant possessiveness over me. How dare he ask me those questions when he won't even claim me as his.

"For your information, not that it matters since we aren't together, these are mine. I buy them in bulk, and they are my go-to lounge-wear when I want to be comfortable."

His face finally softens, realizing there won't be some random man popping out from my bedroom.

I'm about to walk away when Titus grabs me by the arm, slamming me against his chest. "It does matter. Regardless of what we are, you will not take another man into your bed. I forbid it." My head swings back to him, our eyes staring into one another's.

"I am not yours, Titus. Therefore, you have no say in what I do or who I sleep with."

Despite my protest, I belong to him: mind, body and soul. My heart aches for him, and the breath in me hangs on his every word—but still, I will not cower.

Life may have trampled me down, just as it has many before me, but I refuse to let it keep me down.

What I had with Titus was fun, and I enjoyed it while it lasted. But it wasn't meant to be.

Like most things in life, it didn't last.

"Ash—" Titus calls as I move around him, heading out of the kitchen and escaping my new hell.

"Don't. You've made your boundaries clear. We have reverted to being an acquaintance. We live in a reality where we're a breath away yet worlds apart." I close my eyes and smile before turning and walking through the threshold.

I hear him calling my name, but I know I won't stop. I'm in self-preservation mode.

I can't stop.

If I stop, I fall, and if I fall, I break, shattering into a million tiny pieces.

Placing one foot in front of the other, I force myself to walk back to the safety of my room before throwing myself onto the bed.

Covering up with a mountain of pillows and blankets, I close my eyes and whisper to no one, "Wake me up when it's over."

ACTS OF GRACE

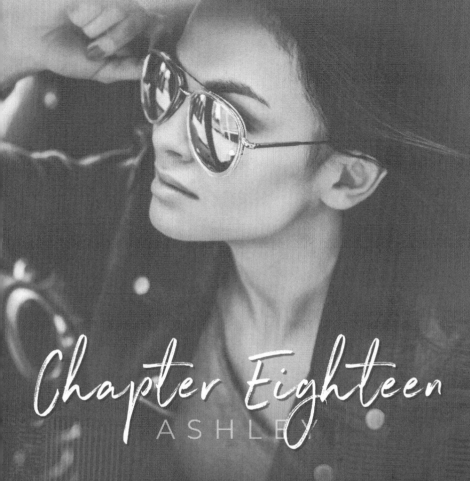

Chapter Eighteen

ASHLEY

Dallas, TX

"**W**hat do you mean you're getting back with Heather? Have you lost your goddamn mind?!" I know I'm yelling at the top of my lungs, but my dear brother has indeed lost his ever-loving mind.

"I know what I'm doing, Ashley. Trust me. It will all make sense in the end." William's hand runs across his face as he blows out a breath of frustration. "It has to be this way. In the meantime, I need you to fly back to California to pick up Harper so she can be here."

My jaw drops, he can't be saying what I think he's saying. "No." I begin pacing in front of him, unable to stand still. "There is no way in hell I'm going to rip Harper from Bella, who's been caring for her like her own, only to bring her back to a poor imitation of a mother." Stopping in front of William, I grab a hold of his hands. "What is this about, William? We left California a little over thirty-two hours ago and by the look of things back there, it seemed as if you were ready to drop on one knee for Bella. What happened?"

"It's done. I've already talked to Bella and told her you were going to pick up Harper later this week." He avoids my gaze, unable to look me in the eye.

"You what?! How did she react? Oh my god, the poor girl!" I resume my pacing once more. What in the world is going on? It's as if I'm in some alternate dimension, not knowing which way is up.

"It doesn't matter how she reacted. What matters is how things will be in the end." He spits out his words as if they're somehow truth.

"Um, sorry to break it to you, but women don't operate that way. If you think that after this stunt you're pulling, Bella will readily forgive you..." I laugh sardonically, shaking my head in disgust. "You're sorely mistaken."

He rolls his eyes before cracking his neck, the tension radiating off of him and slamming straight into me. "Thank you, Ashley, for your valuable advice and for helping me out yet again. Harper trusts you and I knew that if I couldn't pick her up, it had to be you."

"You're lucky I love you both." I mumble under my breath as I exit his study. "Otherwise, you'd be left high and dry in this mess you're concocting."

As I walk back to my room in William's Dallas home, my thoughts go back to Bella. I was talking to her not two nights ago about how much I thought she and William complimented each other.

She's going to be distraught and I'm not sure there's anything I can do about it.

William left so he could go to his court hearing with his ex, and I came back because I wanted to start looking for apartments. I can only imagine what Bella was thinking when she heard from William and his newfound affinity for his ex.

If that psychopath is moving in with us, then I need to find an apartment sooner rather than later.

Titus

"Are you sure?" I'm staring at the team tailing Brad. We're on a face call and none of those fuckers dare look me in the eye right now. They know they've fucked up. They lost their mark.

They lost their *fucking* mark.

"Yes, boss," Mario speaks up while the other cowards hang back. "He was last seen inside of the Dallas airport. With the new COVID protocols for flying, our men got held up by the feds. It took us a while to get through processing and the men waiting outside said they never saw him leave the terminal."

"You are men of WRATH. There should be no excuses. Find him. NOW!" I end the call, slamming my fist onto the wooden desk.

This is unbelievable.

There's a knock at my door and Hudson pops his head in, followed by William. I have no doubt Ren would be here too if it weren't for his taking a job up north in order to avoid William.

"What's the problem?" William sits across from me in one of the leather chairs while Hudson rummages through my bar cart.

"I suppose it's time you found out. Brad disappeared again and the last time he disappeared, he somehow came into contact with your mother."

William's body stiffens as Hudson approaches my desk with three tumblers full of Scotch.

William is the first to swipe a glass, "Just in time."

"I figured we'd need a little something to take the edge off. I assume everyone heard from our local PD, right?"

I nod, taking my glass and bringing it to my lips for a sip. "Yes." I nod toward William. "Who knew your mother was not only an escape artist but a murderer."

William cringes as Hudson shakes his head. "That's low, brother. I wouldn't even joke like that, and that's saying something."

It's true. Hudson is usually the one cracking all the crass, over the top jokes, but I can't help it. I'm in a shit mood after Ashley's ex pulled yet another disappearing act.

"*Escape artist.*" William whispers, more to himself than to anyone in the room.

"Ohhhhh, I see what you're getting at." Hudson's lips turn up as his head bobs up and down.

"What in the," I look back and forth between the two men, narrowing my eyes as the facts come together. "You guys think that Brad and your mother are scheming something together. Question is, what?"

"What, indeed." William smiles. "What could have our mother surfacing to the land of the living? We all thought she was dead, another victim of our father's attacker."

"From where I'm sitting, she's either the attacker or has

somehow miraculously escaped their grasp, only to seek out Ashley's loser boyfriend."

William closes his eyes, flinging his head back into the chair. "I fear you're right. Not only did my mother run Bella off the road, killing her mother, she's also quite possibly the one who murdered our father."

"Hey, look at the bright side." Hudson places his hand on William's shoulder. "You'd be a shoo-in for Jerry Springer if you ever wanted your fifteen minutes of fame."

I chuckle. Despite the dire circumstances surrounding his family, even William has to admit, that's pretty damn funny.

"Ha ha." William mumbles into his rocks glass. "Until we know for certain what the ties are between mother dearest and Brad, let's keep it under wraps and away from the girls. There's no reason to alert Ashley or Bella about this until we have solid facts."

I nod, agreeing with his assessment. The last thing I want is for Ashley focusing on the trauma of her childhood while her ex tries to weasel his way back to her. "For all we know, Brad could've been the one who sought your mother out, trying to use her as leverage to get back with Ashley."

Hudson arches a brow while his hands rub at his jawline. "Anything is possible. But the guy didn't strike me as a mastermind though. I think since both of you are so deeply vested in your women, it's hard for you to see things clearly. If it's okay with everyone, I'm going to add myself to Brad's case."

William's brows push together as I stare a hole right through Hudson's head.

William clears his throat, almost choking on his drink. "What do you mean 'vested in your women'?"

Hudson pales, looking as if he's just seen a ghost.

He's about to *be* a damn ghost if he doesn't fix his slip-up.

"Um, all I meant was that you're clearly vested in how Bella will react, and Titus is clearly vested in Ashley's well-being since you tasked him with watching out for her." Hudson's lips roll in and his eyes bounce in their sockets between William and me.

"Ah," William responds but his brows remain furrowed. "I see." Switching his focus onto me, he blindsides me with a question. "You'd tell me if there was something going on between you and Ashley, right Titus?"

Taking a massive gulp of Scotch, I slam my tumbler down onto the desk before answering. "Brother, I can assure you, Ashley and I have nothing going on right now."

Technically that's true. Right at this very moment, Ashley and I have nothing going on...

William's eyes narrow further, his head bobbing up and down slowly. "Okay. Be sure to let me know if that ever changes."

And just like that, the gauntlet has been thrown down.

If I was hanging on to a sliver of hope, wondering whether Ashley and I could have our cake and eat it too, the answer is clearly and unequivocally *NO*.

We cannot.

ACTS OF GRACE

Chapter Nineteen
ASHLEY

My palms are sweating and my stomach is churning. I know that I'm going to get heat for what I'm about to do, but I'm in fact a grown woman and I don't need my brother's approval to move into a new apartment.

Yes, I know things are crazy right now and that my security team is probably calling him right this very moment, ratting me out, but I don't care.

It's time I moved into a place of my own.

Florida was temporary, and the first time I lived away from William. College gave me the perfect excuse to move out, but now that I've graduated, all I have is my newly asserted independence and the desire to stay out of William's drama.

It's been five days since he decided to get back with Heather and the last straw was seeing Bella's broken heart on full display as I picked up Harper last night.

The poor girl looked like she hadn't eaten or slept in days. I wish I could've offered her more insight as to what my bull-headed brother was thinking, but I have no clue.

Doing the only thing I can think of, I pull out my phone and dial Bella's best friend, Cassie.

The phone rings twice before a cheerful voice answer, "Hello?"

"Hi Cassie. This is Ashley Hawthorne, William's—"

"Sister! Yes, Bella has told me so much about you. Is everything okay? God, is Bella's dad okay?"

"Yes, he's doing as expected with minor improvements every day. We're holding out hope that he'll make a full recovery."

"Oh, good. Now that I can breathe, what can I do for you?"

I wince, knowing that I'm probably about to step over the line here since we've only ever really talked in passing but I know Bella needs this. "So, I'm not sure if Bella's told you what happened with my brother..."

I hear her groan on the other end of the line, "What has the buffoon done now?"

I chuckle, at least I won't have to explain my brother's irrational mood swings. It seems she knows them well. "He's broken things off with Bella and when I picked up Harper last night, Bella didn't look like she was doing too hot. I was thinking if I offered up the jet, maybe you could pay her a visit? She's really in need of a friend right now, and I'm afraid I just wouldn't fit the bill, since I'm the offender's sister and all."

"Ugh. Why are men so damn stupid?! Of course I'll go visit, and I don't need the jet, thank you very much. I don't want anything to do with Re—I mean William."

I cock a brow... was she about to say Ren?

Deciding to ignore the slip up, I let it go, because come on... we've all fallen for a WRATH man and saying anything would be the pot calling the kettle black.

"You're such a good friend. If only I could be so lucky as to find myself a Cassie." I chuckle into the line, joking but not really.

"Well, there's always room for one more. I have to warn you, we don't sugar coat, can be crass, and love to bust balls, but we will always have your back."

My smile could not be any bigger, "Thank you. I'll definitely take you up on that. When you're both back in Dallas, we should get together for a girls' night."

"Yesssss, margaritas and whiskey! There's a new bar I've been dying to try out. It's a martini lounge where they have live blues music."

"That sounds amazing! Okay, it's on when you get back. Keep me posted on how Bella's doing when you're out there, and thanks again. You're the best!"

"Don't I know it." She laughs into the line before disconnecting.

With a huge smile on my face, I step out of my car and into what will be my new home.

I'm standing in front of the premier high-rise in downtown Dallas, about to meet with my realtor and what were once nerves is now full-blown excitement.

The cool lines of the all glass building perfectly emphasizes the name of the building, The Glass House. It has a rooftop bar and lounge area that overlooks the entire downtown scene, complete with a suspended infinity pool.

I cannot wait to invite Bella and Ashley over for some sun and fun!

"Ms. Hawthorne?" A tall blond man, with a killer smile beams down at me. "Are you ready to tour your new home?"

I nibble on my bottom lip, feeling as if I'm about to do something naughty, but reveling in it nonetheless. "Why, yes. Yes, I am."

Titus

"She did what?!"

The man in front of me, lowers his face, staring at the ground as if it were the most fascinating thing he's seen all year. "She met with a man, about six-three, blond, tailored suit. They went up into a sky-rise in downtown and they haven't come out yet. Our men are running a background on who he is and what ties he could have with Ashley."

I pick up the receiver on my desk and dial Ashley's number. "They're taking too long. I'll just call the source directly."

"Sir, do you think that's wise? She'll know we've been following her, and she doesn't take kindly to her privacy being infringed upon."

I scoff, "You think she doesn't already know she has a full detail on her at all times? She's essentially the princess of WRATH securities. There's no way she didn't know whatever she's doing right now wouldn't get back to us."

He refuses to answer, because he knows I'm right. It's sad, but in a way, it's a price you have to pay when you're part of the family. WRATH does a lot of good, but we also make a lot of enemies.

Not only do we provide services to the social elite, we also do extraction and other not so savory jobs for cartels and mafia families.

That in turn, earns us a spot on many shit lists.

I growl, slamming the phone down on its cradle. "She isn't picking up."

Visions of Ashley rolling around in bed with some blond asshole flash before me, making me want to hurl something.

"Find out where she is in the building and get her on the line."

My man just stands there, mouth open, in pure disbelief.

Don't they know by now that I'll go through whatever means necessary to keep her safe? We don't know anything about this man.

Standing, I press my knuckles to the desk and glare. "I meant now."

"Yes, sir. Of course, sir." As he turns to exit, I can't help but hear Ashley's last words to me, '*I am not yours, Titus. You have no say in what I do or who I sleep with.*'

Like hell, I don't.

Chapter Twenty
ASHLEY

I just put down the deposit to my very own apartment in the city, and I can't stop myself from smiling. I'm standing outside on the balcony, taking in the expansive downtown view.

Gah. I can't believe I hadn't done this sooner.

"Enjoying the view?" Jacob, the realtor, comes out onto the balcony extending his hand and offering me my very own set of keys.

Without thinking, I reach for them and pull him into a hug. "Thank you so much. You have no idea how much this means to me."

"Get. Your. Fucking. Hands. Off." A familiar voice growls

through clenched teeth.

Jacob drops his arms as if I were on fire, and I don't blame him one bit. Titus sounds like he's about to murder someone, and with just one look at him, you know that's not far from the truth. His jaw keeps clicking, his fists are clenched, and his nostrils are flared.

"Titus. What are you doing here?" I'm not about to cower just because he caught me hugging a man. It's not like I was about to jump Jacob's bones. Besides, he made it clear we aren't together.

"I could ask you the very same thing." Titus narrows his eyes, looking between Jacob and me.

The poor realtor grimaces. "It's clear you two have some talking to do." He turns back to me, offering me a small wave and not daring to touch me in front of Titus. "Ashley, congratulations again. Call me if you have any problems settling in."

I give him my megawatt smile, truly grateful for his help in securing a nearly impossible to snag apartment.

Titus stalks toward me as soon as Jacob steps inside. "Mind telling me what you were doing with that realtor?" His words are low, but the threat is palpable.

"Isn't it obvious?" I dangle my new set of keys and grin. I don't bother asking how he knew Jacob was a realtor. He's a man of WRATH. They practically know everything, and what they don't know they find out.

It's annoying.

Titus snatches the keys from my hand before grabbing me by the waist and swooping me inside.

"Put me down, Titus! And give me back my keys!" He's thrown me over his shoulder so now I'm hanging upside down, my fists pounding into his back as I try and get back on my own two feet.

"I'll put you down when I'm good and ready." Titus walks us into the sleek open planned kitchen, and I drool. It even looks pretty while hanging upside down.

Seriously, the white quartz and stainless-steel appliances are accentuated by the brass hardware—the jewelry to a home.

I can't stop staring.

Finally coming to a stop, Titus rights me, setting me down on top of the kitchen island, my black sundress contrasting against the white stone.

"We're going to start with why. Why, Ashley?" His eyes burrow deep into me, seeking understanding for something that shouldn't even have to be asked.

"Why? Why not? I'm twenty-one years old. I just finished undergrad, about to start on my masters, had a horrible breakup, feel like a third wheel at my overprotective brother's house, and oh yeah, I'm single. S. I. N. G. L. E. Single. That means I don't have to run my major life choices by anyone other than myself."

Titus cracks his neck and rolls his shoulders before focusing his eyes back on me, frustration evident in his face. "That's not what I was asking." He pauses, as if his reasoning is now somehow clear. *Yeah, it's not.* "Why, Ashley? Why were you hugging that man?"

My body involuntarily jerks back as I scoff. "Oh my god. That's what you want to know? I've just made a major life choice without consulting my brother or anyone on the WRATH team, and what you want to know is why I was hugging my realtor?"

Titus doesn't look amused. His face remains unaffected, waiting for my response.

Rolling my eyes, I lay back onto the counter placing my

weight on my forearms. "I was excited. Overjoyed. Elated. Ecstatic. On cloud nine." Blowing out a breath of irritation, I finally give him what he wants to know. "I did what anyone would do when they're overwhelmed with gratitude. It meant nothing beyond that. I'm not into him and he's not into me."

Titus' hands fall to my thighs, squeezing them hard before prying my legs apart and settling between them. "You may have wanted nothing to do with him, but I can assure you, he definitely wanted something to do with you. He's a man, Ashley. And you," he grabs my hips, sliding me to him, my apex reaching the bulge in his pants making me groan. "You, my precious little treasure, are a sight to behold."

My hips act of their own accord, rolling my core onto his ridge, seeking that delicious friction I love so much.

His growl is feral and the look in his eyes is pure molten lava.

Despite knowing that I should relent, giving in to what he and I both want, I can't. I've never been one to leave well enough alone, so I take what he's given me and fuel it. "And? So what if he wants me. I'm not with anyone. Nobody has the right to stop me if I wanted to accept his advances."

"Ashley Hawthorne," his hand reaches my neck, squeezing as he pulls my face to his, "you are mine and you will not allow another man to touch you, or so help me god, I will not be responsible for ripping them to shreds, scattering their body parts to serve as a warning. Do not touch what's mine."

My hand reaches down the front of his slacks, grabbing a hold of his very aroused cock, and squeeze. "If I'm yours, then you are *mine*. And I'm not responsible for ripping apart anyone who dares touch what is mine."

At my words, he pulses in my hand, making my pussy clench right along with it.

Titus' hands slide to the back of my head, his fingers fisting my hair and tilting my head back before his mouth descends on my neck, sucking and biting at the tender flesh.

"Yes, *min skatt*. I am yours," he grits out, his voice thick with desire, melting whatever's left of my anger. "And you are mine." His tongue laps at the bruised spot he just bit before licking his way up my jawline and right to my open and panting mouth.

A violent clash of tongues and teeth ferociously lap and nip at each other, wanting to devour the other whole.

My body rises up, molding to his as if we were one in this tangle of limbs and lust.

"I need you." His words are pained, as if he were ashamed of his own desire.

Needing to wash away any of his guilt, I do the only thing I can think of, I give him what he needs.

Sliding off the counter, I drop to my knees and lower my gaze. In this moment and every moment moving forward, I want to be the only thing he wants, the only thing he needs.

"Yes, sir. Let me please you."

His big hand reaches down to my chin, pinching it with his fingers and lifting my face toward his, "*Min skatt*, know this— you are mine and that means that I'll never let harm come to you. You are precious to me, and whatever we do in the throes of passion is just as much for you as it is for me. You are mine to treasure. Mine to pleasure. Mine to adore."

My eyes water at the devotion in his eyes. I can feel him, his heart and soul—all pouring through, right into his words.

"Say it, Ashley. Repeat those words so I know you understand."

"Yes. I am yours to treasure, yours to pleasure, and yours to adore." My mouth dries at the way he's staring. He may not say the three words I want to hear, but this is as much a declaration of love as I've ever heard it.

My calloused and damaged man, declaring his devotion to me the only way he knows how, pleading his loyalty only to me.

"Rise." Titus' commands and my body does as it's told. "Bend over."

His large hand presses against my back, pushing me chest down onto the cold white stone of the island.

With one rough pull, Titus rips my dress in two, throwing the black fabric to the side.

My hard little nipples brush against the cold stone and I gasp, feeling Titus' hands grip my waist from behind.

"You've been a naughty little girl, Ashley." His fingers dig deep into my flesh as he thrusts my bare ass back into him, the sensation of his slacks rubbing up against my pussy, driving me wild and serving as a tease of what's to come.

He lowers his body to mine, the fabric of his shirt rubbing against the exposed flesh of my back.

"Do you know what happens to naughty girls?" Titus whispers into the soft skin of my neck.

"No, Daddy." I respond, my words coming out more of a mewl.

"They get spanked." I hear the clanking of his belt and his breathing deepening just like mine. "Place your hands on the counter. Now."

A thrill runs through me, making my whole body quiver.

"Yes, Daddy."

His commands strike something deep within me, driving me wild, and making me drip with desire.

I revel in being at his mercy, letting him take control as he pushes me to my limits, seeking out every ounce of my pleasure.

"Agh," I moan as his leather belt lands on my left cheek before he's rubbing at the stinging flesh.

"That was for letting him touch you." Titus brings his palm to my right cheek, rubbing the globe before issuing another crack of his leather belt. "That was for thinking you could ever belong to someone other than me. You are mine, Ashley Hawthorne." His fingers rub over my slick folds, no doubt noticing how wet he's made me. "This belongs to me."

He brings down his belt, issuing a quick but brutal slap to my pussy—the action making me moan in ecstasy as the combination of pain and pleasure dance together in what could only be described as the perfect symphony.

"Titus, please." I beg, needing more of him. Needing all of him.

"Please what, *min skatt?*" His growl is feral as he grinds his length against my bare ass, soaking his pants with my arousal.

"I need you inside me."

"This? Do you need this?" He slips his gloriously thick fingers inside of me and I groan, bucking my ass in the air like the needy girl that I am.

"More, please. I need more."

He frees himself running the wide head of his cock up and down my slit.

"Fuck, you're so wet, baby. I want to watch your little cunt swallow me whole."

His words become reality as he impales himself into me, making me arch my back as I cry out his name in relief.

"That's right, baby. It's *my* name on your lips." His hand snakes its way up my torso and onto my throat, his fingers wrapping around it in a possessive hold, all while thrusting himself in and out of my aching core. "It is me. Me who sets

187

your soul on fire, bringing you to the pinnacle of pleasure and making you soar among the stars."

"Yes, oh my god, yes!" Everything he's said is true. All of it. His pace picks up as his body slams into mine with enough force to make my whole body shake.

"*Min skatt*. My treasure." The hand on my hip trails down to my clit, his fingers rubbing tiny circles onto the bundle of nerves. "I know this to be true because that is what you do to me. I burn for you, and only you."

Tears I had no idea I was holding back leak from my face. My tortured and calloused man is speaking from his heart, and his words are nothing but sheer poetry.

"Come with me, baby. Let's dance among the stars." And with one final thrust, we fall.

ACTS OF GRACE

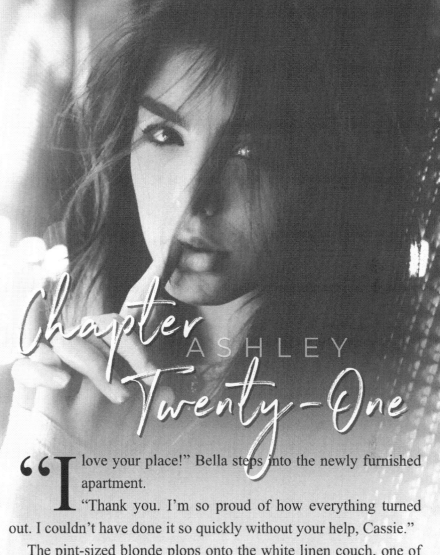

Chapter Twenty-One

ASHLEY

"I love your place!" Bella steps into the newly furnished apartment.

"Thank you. I'm so proud of how everything turned out. I couldn't have done it so quickly without your help, Cassie."

The pint-sized blonde plops onto the white linen couch, one of the pieces she helped me pick out for my new place. "You're so welcome. It's so much fun shopping on someone else's dime. Especially since the turn around was only a couple of weeks. Nothing racks up the fees like rush deliveries."

"Ugh, don't remind me." I shake my head as I pour all of us a glass of rosé. "But, hey, I'd pay it all over again if it meant not having to shack up with William anymore."

"He's not that bad. Bella blushes as she places a hand over her glass, signaling she's not having any. "And thanks, but I'm not having any today. My stomach hasn't been right since the Thai we had last night." Her hand flies up to her mouth as if she's going to hurl."

"Of course! Let me get you some fizzy water. Hopefully that helps settle your stomach."

It's been about a week since Bella's been back in town, and Aiden was discharged from the hospital. He's made immense progress and he's even up and talking, only needing the assistance of a nurse for routine therapy.

Cassie takes a sip of her drink, before asking what we both want to know. "So, how are things with William since you got back?"

Bella flings herself back into the white egg chair. "Ummm, Dad doesn't know about William and me if that's what you're asking. We're waiting until he's stable before telling him."

"I still can't believe you forgave him for that stunt he pulled with Heather. I know they weren't actually together, but still."

"I hate to agree with Cassie, since William is my brother, but she's right. I can't believe it either." I place a glass of sparkling water in front of her, noticing her extra pale complexion. "You sure you're okay? You're looking sort of clammy."

Bella reaches for her drink, taking a small sip. "I'm fine, it's probably just a mild case of food poisoning. And as far as forgiving William, trust me... I'm still making him work for it." She bites at her bottom lip and smirks.

It's my turn for my stomach to roll. Holding up a hand, I plead, "Stop. No further details necessary. I'm more than okay with you two being together but I draw the line at hearing my brother's sexual proclivities."

Bella and Cassie both let out a cackle, "Okay, let's switch topics then." They both peer at me with a devilish grin. "So, how's Titus doing?"

My face heats, "Titus? Why would I know anything about Titus?"

"Uh-huh." Bella shakes her head. "You can't fool us. We see how you two look at each other. And don't think we've missed Titus' things lying about the apartment either."

Cassie smirks, "Hey, it's not like we can blame you. WRATH men *are* in a class all their own."

I chuckle, "I take it that means things between you and Ren are going well?"

Cassie beams as she flips through one of my style magazines, "Can't say that I have any complaints. Well, other than my mom trying to get Ren and I to walk down the aisle already. I swear, that woman is more obsessed with Ren than I am."

She's grinning ear to ear, no doubt thinking of Bella's uncle, one of the five men of WRATH.

I sigh into my drink, "Admittedly, I'm a bit jealous. You two get to openly be with your men."

"Hey, I still have to hide it from my dad. We're afraid that the information will hinder his recovery. There's so much we're having to keep from him, it feels as if I'm constantly walking on eggshells. I can't even imagine what he'd do if he found out about my mom, or your mom for that matter." Bella tips her glass toward me, her head shaking in disapproval.

My brows furrow, confused at her words. "My father, you mean. He's the one that had the affair with your mom."

"Sure, that's only the first part. The real kicker is how your mom found out, got jealous and tried to kill us by running my mother and me off the road three years ago."

My jaw drops and chest tightens. *What the hell is she talking about?*

Bella's face turns chalk white as Cassie gives her the side eye. "Oh my god, you didn't know, did you?"

Cassie smacks Bella on the thigh. "Her mouth hanging wide open would be a clear indication she was clueless. Here, let me pour you another drink while Bella spills the beans. Something your man, or your brother at the very least, should have done already."

"I'm so sorry, Ashley. I though you would've known by now. Specially with how close you and Titus have been."

"Clearly, we're not." I groan, knowing I shouldn't give her attitude. She's not the one who's at fault. "I'm sorry. Please tell me what my brother and Titus both think I can't handle. That's the only reason I see them keeping something like this from me."

Bella winces, "Well, you already know about the car accident that killed my mom three years ago. The police reached out to the men and told them they found the car that ran us off the road. It was recovered from the river when the police were doing a dive, searching for a jumper."

Cassie does the sign of the cross before bringing her thumb to her lips as she mumbles, "I can't believe people are still jumping off that bridge." Her eyes look between Bella and me. "I'm sorry, continue."

"No we get it. They need to do something about the rails." I make a mental note to write a letter to our mayor and tack it on right below reaming my brother for his latest fuck-up.

Bella nods before continuing. "Yes, well, they found the car and were able to figure out who the driver was. Turns out your mom bought the car from a cash lot. The owner was able to identify her and everything."

My hands fly to my stomach, its flipping making me feel as if I'm about to vomit. "But why? All this time we thought she'd been a victim of my father's killer."

Cassie's brows raise, practically hitting her hair line. "Isn't it obvious. Seems to me, she found out about your dad cheating with Bella's mom and she wanted to end her husband's lover."

"I'm going to be sick." I stand only to pace along the expansive glass windows to the outside. "I mean, I guess it makes sense, I just never wanted to see it." Stopping, I place my hands on my knees and dry heave. My god, you don't think *she* killed my father, do you?"

I look toward my two best friends, hoping they can tell me I'm wrong, but all I see is sadness and pity.

"I'm not ruling it out." Bella's melancholy voice hits me right in the chest.

"If this is all true then, my mother not only killed your mother, but she also killed my father."

Cassie steps behind me, handing me a cold wet towel. "Let's not jump to conclusions. The men are looking into the connections now."

Whipping back around at Cassie, I can't help but lash out, "*You* knew too?"

Taking two steps back, Cassie slowly nods. "I'm sorry. We thought for sure you'd also known."

"Clearly not." Placing the cold rag to my face, I take in a deep breath and try to make sense of what I've just learned. "So what are they planning now that they've discovered this information? Are they looking for my mother? Why isn't she in custody already."

Bella sinks back into her chair, chewing on her bottom lip.

"They're trying to locate her but with everything else they have going on with William's case being finalized and my dad's recovery, everything has sort of been stagnant."

My jaw ticks. I'm not only upset at the fact that the men have kept this information from me, but the fact that they haven't been acting on it digs the dagger in even deeper.

Had I known, I would be doing everything possible to find that wretched human being.

I was never close to my mother, a woman who was always drunk or on some sort of happy pill that never really made her all that happy. Calling her mother would be too generous a description.

When she went missing after our father's death, I was upset but not devastated. I was closer to my dad, so it was no shock I was grieving his loss over hers.

The way I found him, laying in a pool of his own blood, detracted from whatever sadness I could have felt for my absentee mother.

"I'm so sorry, Ashley." Bella is no in front of me with both arms extended.

Taking her up on her hug, I let my new best friends surround me with love. "No. Thank you for telling me. I appreciate you both beyond words."

It's true. Had these women not come into my life, I'd be clueless.

With a brother who's extremely overprotective and a lover who doesn't communicate, I'm walking blind while everyone around me has x-ray vision.

"Of course we'd tell you. Remember, we never sugar coat things and always tell it like it is. But we will *always* have your back. No matter what." Cassie beams, repeating what she told me when I first joined their tribe of two.

"Yup, we're ride or die, bitches!" Bella shouts as Cassie and I laugh before shouting in unison, "Ride or die!"

Titus

She hasn't answered my calls and I know she's alone in her apartment. The girls left about an hour ago and Ashley's yet to give me the all-clear.

Fuck it. I'm going up anyway.

As I'm riding up the elevator, my head is going through all the possible things that could've pissed Ashley off.

She's not some delicate flower I have to tend to every hour of every day, and I haven't done anything different for her to be upset about.

I shake my head, groaning at the absurdity of my thoughts.

What the hell is wrong with me.

I've gone from being a no relationship, no feelings type of man to someone who pre-games possible fights with their lover.

The elevator door opens and the first thing I see stops me dead in my tracks.

Ashley at her door, in a little black dress, talking to Jacob.

No. Just, no.

Walking past the realtor, I walk through the threshold and grab Ashley by the waist, bringing her small frame to mine and landing a very intimate kiss on her pouty lips.

She's mine and if this proverbial pissing on a fire hydrant doesn't do the trick, maybe a fist to the face will clear things up.

Ashley clears her throat, "Jacob, you've met Titus, my *friend*." She gives me the side eye as she over-annunciates 'friend.'

The asshole has the balls to smirk at the status Ashley has given us. "Yes, I had the pleasure of meeting him the day you signed your lease. Like I was saying before we were interrupted, there's a weekly happy hour every Friday. It's up on the deck and every tenant over twenty-one is welcome. Since you just had your birthday, I thought we could include you in this month's festivities."

Ashley squeals, "Oh, I'd love that! Is it okay if I bring a couple of friends?" Mr. Slick eyes me, hesitating with his response, but Ashley cuts him off before he's had a chance to say anything. "Bella and Cassie would love to be my plus ones!"

My brows push together, not happy with what she's said. The girls aren't twenty-one yet, and there's no telling what sort of jackals are waiting to prey on the young and inexperienced.

I'm about to say something when Slick cuts it. "Ah, yes. They are more than welcome." His seedy smile is on full display, no doubt thinking of all the things he could do to lure and trap Ashley and her friends.

Yeah, good luck with that buddy. These ladies are the Women of WRATH. They are queens in their own right and there isn't a man in our team that wouldn't die to protect them, let alone keep them away from predators like this fool.

Having heard enough of his bullshit, I decide to cut this conversation short. "Right, well now that you've given out your invitation, Ashley and I would like to get to our evening."

Ashley looks up at me, murder gleaming in her baby blues. "Yes, Titus and I have *a lot* to discuss."

Well, fuck.

ACTS OF GRACE

Chapter Twenty-Two
ASHLEY

The nerve of this man, showing up like he owns me.

Closing the door on Jacob, I turn to face Titus. "What goes on in that mind of yours? On what planet do you think it's okay for you to come to my home, act like my man, and piss all over your perceived territory without giving me any of the benefit that would come along with it?"

Titus' brows hit his hairline. "Whoa there. First of all, you *are* mine and I am yours. We've already established that. Second of all, this," he grabs my hips, pulling back to him, "is off limits to any other man, so yeah. I get to claim you publicly, despite you calling me your *friend.*"

I push myself free from his hold, "You're right. I shouldn't call you friend. That term would be too kind."

He has the audacity to scoff, "What are you going on about, woman. What in the world could I have done to get you all bent out of shape?"

His words only serve as fuel, angering me and wanting to kick him out for his ignorance. Closing my eyes, I let out a slow breath. "You, Titus Eirik Bond, have been keeping things from me. Things that a *friend* would never keep to themselves."

Like a garage door coming down, I see the shutter of indifference taking over Titus' face. No longer do I see the confused and frustrated man who I thought was my partner. He is long gone, and in his place is the ever-stoic Titus Bond.

"That's what I thought. Nothing to say now that you've been called out. Well let me make things clearer, when you know something that could very much affect a friend's well-being, you come clean about it. Keeping it from them can only mean a lack of apathy."

There he is, his face has come roaring back to life. "Bullshit!" He slams a fist into the wall before heading deeper into the apartment. "Everything I kept from you was to keep you safe, not because I lack feelings for you. If anything, I have too many damn feelings for you. I can't stop thinking about you. All day long, it sneaks into everything I do. For fucks sake, I can't even go up a damn elevator without thinking about how you're feeling."

He's headed into the closet, rummaging through some boxes. *What in the world?*

"Okay. If you feel so much for me, then how could you keep vital information from me? How would knowing that my mother is still alive be putting me in danger?"

Titus doesn't respond to me, instead he keeps rummaging

through the boxes in my closet, mumbling to himself. "Hudson was right, WRATH women are crazy."

"Excuse me... did you just call me crazy?"

Titus pulls some papers out of a small white box before storming toward me. "Yes. I fucking did."

His strong arms pick me up, throwing me over his shoulder as he carries me to bed before throwing me onto the feather lined duvet.

Before I can say anything, Titus has sat himself at the foot of the bed. His entire body is rigid, not a hint of humor to be seen as he extends his arm out, handing me the papers he's just retrieved.

My hand hesitantly reaches out, scared at whatever revelation they hold inside.

MARISSA HAWTHORNE, DECEASED, remains found along a jogging trail in Dallas, Texas.

"What is this?" My voice cracks as I ask Titus to explain.

"It's the report we obtained three years ago. It confirmed a fake narrative that your mother was dead."

"But she's not, right?" My face scrunches together as I try and make sense of the report. "Unless she killed my dad, then killed Bella's mom by running them off the road... and then died?"

Titus grabs my legs and drags me to him, "I wanted you to see why we stopped looking into her before I continue with what's been going on now and why we want to you keep you safe."

I cock a brow, his proximity soothing the ache in my chest and making me a little more forgiving. "Okay. Explain."

"So you already put two and two together. It's quite possible that your mother murdered your father and then ran Bella and her mom off the road. What was new information was that Marissa is still alive."

"Okay, now I'm even more confused."

Titus places his index finger on my lips, silencing me. Too bad I'm not in the mood. Opening my mouth wide, I take his finger and bite. "Talk, Titus."

He shakes his head and gives me a sad smile. "Remember I told you the gun used on Bella's car was the same one used in your father's murder?"

Sucking in air, the horror sets in. "Not only did my psychopath mother kill my father and Bella's mother, she's now trying to kill Bella too?"

Titus cups my face in his hands before pressing a kiss to my forehead. "*Min skatt*, there's more."

I squeeze my eyes shut, regretting having ever brought this up. "Just rip it off with one clean pull."

"Last night we found out how William's ex kept winning all of their cases in court."

My brows squeeze together as my head begins to pound. "What does William's gold-digging ex have to do with our mother, or Bella for that matter?"

"We're not sure of the reason behind the connection yet, only that there is one. Marissa is in a relationship with one of the judges and has been giving Heather assurances that she'd win against William." My mouth is hanging wide open. "This sordid tale is something straight out of daytime soap opera."

Titus chuckles, but the smile doesn't quite reach his eyes. "I wish that were all, but there's even more fucked up shit happening behind the scenes."

"Oh, come on. How much have you guys been keeping from me and the girls? I know they don't have a clue about the connection between Bella's tires and my dad's murder. They would've told me if they did."

"At least those assholes kept their word about some of the things." Titus mumbles to himself as he runs the palm of his hand across his face. "There's only one other thing. It's about Brad, your ex. Like Heather, he's also been in contact with your mother. We aren't sure what the connection is yet, but I'm guessing it's probably the same reason Marissa was working the Heather angle."

My eyes shoot open, the shock on my face evident based on Titus' look of pity. "I just don't understand. What in the world could Brad and Heather have to do with our mother?"

"We aren't sure yet, but I've been working on a source. We have a full team working on piecing everything together and I promise I'll tell you what I know when I learn of it. For now, we've doubled security and have done everything to keep you ladies safe."

"Us ladies?"

"Yes, you, Bella, Cassie, and Alyssa."

"Who's Alyssa?"

"Hudson's stepsister. She's moved in with him while she goes to college here. We're not sure who else has been pulled into this scheme or why, so for now, the ladies of WRATH are on lockdown."

Lockdown. Ugh. The word sounding oppressive to my ears.

"Are lockdowns absolutely necessary?"

"You aren't a prisoner, Ashley. You're free to go about your normal activities. The only exception is that you will be closely monitored in everything you do outside of your home."

I roll my eyes and blow out a breath. "So what you're saying is that things are operating per usual."

Titus chuckles, "Can you blame us? I leave you alone for one day and you've not only turned on me, but you're entertaining a blond man at your door."

"Ha! You make it seem as if I were flirting with my realtor. And don't think you're off the hook. You still haven't explained why you've kept things from me."

Titus lays me back down onto the bed, crawling over me so that our faces are a breath apart. "One, He *was* flirting. Two, I did tell you why. At first, we simply didn't know. And once we found out your mother was still alive, we all agreed it would be best if we didn't stress you out with the information. You were already so devastated with what happened in Florida, telling you about this would've only added to your stress. Not something any of us wanted to do."

I reach up, taking his bottom lip between my teeth and sucking at the juicy flesh before releasing it with a pop. "No more. From now on you can't hide anything from me. Not if you want us to continue having whatever it is that we have."

Titus grabs the back of my thighs, lifting me up and smacking my ass, "Deal. And what we have is each other. I am yours, unconditionally and I'll always do what I think is in your best interest, whether you see it that way or not."

"For your information, keeping things is *not* in my best interest. When I find out about things through my best friends instead of the man I share my body with, I feel like a dumb ass that's been played." I purse my lips and raise a brow, unwilling to let this happen again.

Titus grabs me by the waist while chuckling, flipping me over so my stomach is on the bed. "Understood, little treasure. Those fuckers went against their word and told their women when they said they wouldn't." His big hands trail from my shoulders to my waist before finally latching on to my ass, squeezing the globes in a punishing grip. "Never again, *min skatt*. You will always come first."

My whole body stills at the implication of his words, making my heart catch in my throat. I would *never* ask him to choose between his brotherhood and me.

That's not who I am.

But that fact that he's doing it because he wants to, because he cares for me that much... I'm at a loss for words.

I gasp as his thick fingers slide between my folds, feeling the dampness that lies in waiting. Waiting for his fingers, his tongue, his delicious cock.

"Cat's got your tongue, little treasure?" Titus' voice is thick as one of his hands slides up my abdomen, past the curves of my breasts and ending at my throat. His fingers grip on to the delicate flesh and pull me back to his chest. "Let me make it clear. You are my queen."

Titus fastens something around my neck. "I'm tied to you for life, Ashley Hawthorne. No other will ever do." Turning me around he carries me to the full-length mirror, standing me before him.

A thin platinum chain rests close to my throat, the strand connected by a delicate circle through which
a pendant hangs.

Is this a collar?

My brows push together as I look back at him through the reflection. His words are so at odds at what this thing around my neck symbolizes, aren't they?

Titus fingers trail the length of my collar, his eyes looking on with adoration. "To live in a world devoid of your presence would be to live in a state of death, mourning the loss of my other half. You, Ashley Hawthorne, have consumed every part of me, leaving no cell unturned."

My eyes water and my lip trembles. His words, they're what I've always wanted to hear. He too, is my other half, and after having this time with him, I don't think I could ever survive if something were to ever happen to him.

"Titus, I love you. I've always loved you." My voice cracks, the words sounding surreal to my own ears. These are words I've said a million times in my head, but never out loud.

Gripping my face in his hands, he brings my face to his, hovering his lips over mine, "I've always loved you, *min skatt.* You're my little treasure, the light in my life. Whatever happens, you will always be mine, and I will always be yours."

Needing no further reassurance that this man is my forever, I dive head first into him, his love, and yes, *even his kink.*

ACTS OF GRACE

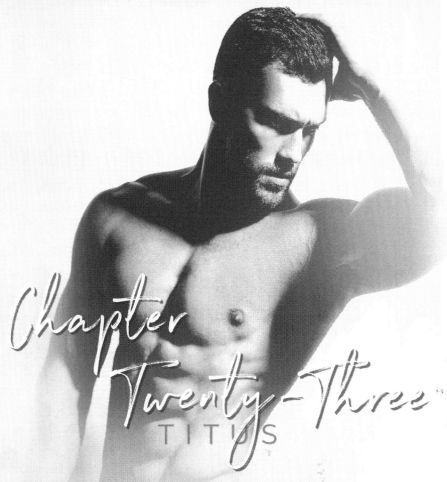

Chapter Twenty-Three
TITUS

The vibrating on the nightstand wakes me up from blissful sleep. It's too damn early for anyone to be calling so it better damn well be an emergency.

My body protests at being pried from its favorite position, wrapped around Ashley. Every part of me begs to stay in bed with her, just a little longer.

The phone which had stopped vibrating starts its annoying buzzing once more and I know that it really must be an emergency.

Rolling out of the warm bed, I see the lit-up screen displaying the caller.

WILLIAM

Fuck. I wonder if he's found out about Ashley and me. If so, then

I'll have to bump up my schedule for coming clean.

Yes, I'd planned to do it sooner rather than later, but not this damn soon.

Walking into the living room, I answer the call. "Hello?"

"Titus, finally."

I chuckle sarcastically into the line, "You do know what time it is, right?"

"Yes, but I just got a call from Marianna who told me the FBI will be heading over to Aiden's later today. They want some more info on his deceased wife, which means they're going to tell him about the cheating and her ties to both of my parents."

Ashley's parents.

"Shit, this has the potential to backfire in a major way. He's still not at one hundred percent since suffering his accident. This is exactly the type of thing that could derail his progress."

"Exactly. I was hoping the team could get together and head over to his place in an hour. That way we could break the news to him ourselves. This type of thing is always better when it comes from someone you know and trust."

Another sarcastic laugh escapes me, "About that, it seems you may have told Bella some of the information on your mother. Weren't we supposed to keep that under wraps until we figured out all the details?"

"Yeah, uh. Oh, do you hear Harper? She's crying. Better go see what she needs."

"Uh-huh. Convenient. See you later, brother." I shake my head as I cut the line, laughing to myself.

That's got to be a new one... Using your baby to get out of explaining things.

Heading back to the bedroom I see Ashley's beautiful face, her long dark hair serving as a halo around her and framing the beautiful contours of her body.

Her abdomen is flat now, but with how we've been going at it, I'd be surprised if she weren't already carrying my seed.

Birth control isn't one-hundred percent effective, is it?

My cock stirs at the idea of filling her once more, claiming her in every way possible, and I'm tempted to keep the men waiting.

I meant what I said last night, she's mine and no other will do.

I plan on making it official once this whole mess with her mother has been figured out.

Grimacing, my mind wanders to what it'll entail and how it can all turn out.

I'll talk to William and come clean.

Ashley and I are, and always will be, together.

Whether he likes it or not.

"Aiden, you really need to hire a full-time nanny," Ren complains. "I can't fill in for Bella all the time."

"Bella can't hold out on me forever. She loves the boys and will be back to her regular self in no time." Aiden waves away Ren's concerns.

I roll my eyes at the absurdity of his statement. If my being with Ashley has taught me anything, it's that WRATH women are stubborn as fuck and if they set their mind to something, there's no shaking them from it.

If Bella has decided she doesn't want to go to college and become a writer, that's how it'll be. Aiden can pitch a fit until he's blue in the face. Won't matter. The WRATH lady has spoken.

William picks up a kolache, trying to act uninterested when most of us know that he and Bella have been together the last couple of months. "What's going on?"

Ren smirks, no doubt catching on to the fact that William is trying to play dumb. "Bella has gone on strike ever since dear old dad over here shut down her dreams of becoming an author," Ren turns toward Aiden again, "You need to bite the bullet, man. Apologize to her and hire a damn nanny. You were going to do that once she started college. So what's the big deal?"

The whole team has managed to crowd around Aiden's kitchen island, scarfing down kolaches and coffee as we watch this shit show unfold before us.

Aiden glares at his little brother, as if giving Ren the stink eye would make him see that he's the one in the wrong. "The big deal is she dropped out of college before she's even begun!" His shouting making his throat vibrate with each word. "If I hire a nanny, she will think that it's okay for her to forgo all of her responsibilities to pursue a fruitless dream."

William sneers, unable to hide how he truly feels about the circus going on before us. "Fruitless? Have you seen her work? She's brilliant. There's no doubt in my mind she could have a successful career as an author if she wished to be one."

Either Aiden is absolutely clueless about what William's outburst could imply, or he's simply choosing to ignore it. "What is this, gang-up-on-Aiden day."

Hudson finally chimes in with some reason. "No. It's keep-it-real-with-Aiden day. Bella told us you were released from Dr. Ansley's care and that means no more sugar-coating things."

Aiden lets out a low whistle, "Well, shit. If you've been sugar-coating things before, I can't wait to hear what you have to say now."

Hudson runs a hand through his hair, nervously shifting his gaze between everyone. "The reason we're here is to talk to you about your wife. Well, more like something involving your wife."

Here it comes...

"You mean my adulterous spouse? By all means, please tell me what could be worse than finding out the woman you've idolized was sleeping with one of your friend's father," Aiden grits out while staring at William.

I let out a breath, knowing it's my turn. "It's not worse, *per se*. It's just news that could be considered shocking."

Aiden waves his hands, motioning me to move on with it. "Well, what is it then? We don't have all day."

I'm about to continue when William holds up a hand, letting me know he wants to be the one to come clean since this is about his mother. It makes sense. That's how I'd want it too if I were in his shoes.

"We found out who the driver was the night of the car accident three years ago. Aiden, before I tell you, you need to understand that the authorities believe it was an intentional hit. The person who ran into your wife and daughter did so with the intent to harm, and most likely kill."

Aiden's expression goes from annoyed to concerned. "You mean to tell me someone set out to hurt my wife and daughter? How the fuck did I not know about this." His features contort into ones of outrage. "When did you find out about this? Is the person still out there?"

A female voice responds in place of William's.

"Oh, she's very much out there. Isn't she, William?" Heather trains her wild gaze on her husband, cocking the revolver nestled in her outstretched hands.

At once, we all turn our eyes toward the madwoman who's begun to pace back and forth in Aiden's kitchen.

"Heather, what are you doing here?" Aiden asks, his brows furrowing in deep confusion.

"You mean they haven't clued you in?" She laughs, waving her gun in the air in a circular motion. "Well, sit down, darlin'. I'm about to fill you in."

While this crazy bitch is laughing it up, staring at William, I silently round the island. As soon as I've cleared her periphery, I lunge from behind, knocking the revolver from her hand and tackling her to the ground.

The men around me act in unison, quickly getting the things we need to secure her meanwhile we figure out what the fuck to do with her.

I drag her to a chair where William and Hudson zip tie her arms and legs.

As soon as she's subdued, I turn toward Aiden. "Where the fuck is your security team, Aiden?"

"I gave them the day off. I'm a fucking SEAL. I don't need a damn security detail," Aiden rebuffs.

"You gave them the day off?! You might not need the security, but Bella and the twins do. For fuck's sake, what would've happened if they were in the room when Heather came in wielding her gun?" William roars, the veins in his neck pulsating wildly.

Bella suddenly steps into the kitchen, rushing toward William. "I'm here. I'm okay. And the twins are over at the neighbors for a play date."

William glares at Aiden over Bella's head, "You got lucky." He takes two steps forward and pulls Bella into an embrace before placing a kiss to her forehead. "I'm so fucking glad you're okay."

I wince at their public display of affection. If we didn't think things were interesting enough already, they're about to be.

"What the hell is going on?" Aiden looks between William and Bella, confused by their PDA.

Heather cackles from her seat, "You didn't know, did you? Daddy's perfect little angel isn't so perfect."

"Shut your mouth, Heather." Bella growls out, before turning toward her father, about to come clean but William beats her to it.

"I'm in love with your daughter, Aiden." William says it so matter-of-factly, and all of the air is sucked from the room.

Welp, there goes any semblance of breaking this nice and easy.

"How fucking sweet," Heather chimes in, breaking the standstill. "Well, fuck you and your happily ever after. Marissa—Oh wait, she goes by Shannon now." Heather rolls her eyes and shakes her head before continuing. "*Shannon* promised me this would be easy and that everything would be okay. She and I were supposed to be on some remote island sipping daiquiris by now, not having a care in the world. But nooooo. William wouldn't take me back because of *this* little bitch." Heather points her head toward Bella as we all stare on watching this lunatic's confession.

"Watch yourself, Heather. You will not talk about Bella like that," William warns her through clenched teeth.

"You can't control me." Heather scoffs. "I will not let you hold me back, William Hawthorne. You screwed me over once with that damn prenup and I will not let you do it to me again."

"Is that what this is about? The prenup?" William laughs

sardonically.

"Yes! If you would have let me walk away with some money, this wouldn't even be happening right now. Once I realized I wasn't going to get anything from you, I had to come back. Otherwise I'd be left with nothing. That's when your genius mother approached me, talking about some hair-brained scheme to clean you out once you and I were back together. Apparently her stash of money had run out and she was in need of replenishing her funds too."

"Fucking money. It all boils down to money and greed. Coveting that which isn't yours to possess." William shakes his head in disgust.

"Of course it's about money. Haven't you been paying attention? Well, the part where your mother killed your father... *that* was more out of blind jealousy. But I mean, someone was threatening to take away her cash cow, so could you really blame her?"

"Yes!" We all shout in unison. How could this woman thing there was any justification for decapitating someone.

"Whatever. Just be glad I didn't try to kill you and Bella, like your mother did with your father and Lucia. Though trashing Bella's car felt pretty damn good."

"That was you?" Bella gasps in surprise at the same time as William shouts, "Of course it was my mother!"

"Yup." Heather pops her P, seemingly unaffected by being handcuffed to a chair.

"Yes to what? You were the one who vandalized Bella's car, or my mother was the one who murdered my father?" William asks what we already presumed to be true.

"Yes to both of those. I shot Bella's tires out with that gun right there." Heather points her head toward the gun inside the plastic bag. "It was a gift from your treacherous mother. Said she couldn't look at it any longer, something about it being the gun she used on your father."

William shares a knowing look with the rest of the team. We had suspected as much and now this vile human has confirmed it.

"I never should have trusted that woman. But she assured me over and over again that she could make it so I could win my hearing and get back into William's good graces." Heather laughs maniacally. "We hadn't counted on William fucking the nanny, though. That definitely threw a wrench in our plans." Heather turns her head to look at Bella. "You dug your heels in real good, didn't you honey."

Bella narrows her eyes at Heather, unable to keep quiet any longer. Don't blame me if you never appreciated what was right in front of you. You were the one who walked away from a life with William and Harper. Throughout this entire breakdown of yours, you haven't even mentioned her once!"

Damn. She's right, though.

"You could have them both for all I care. I just needed the money. Instead, I get a call from the mastermind herself telling me that the jig is up. That there are warrants out for our arrest and she's going into hiding. Do you think the brain decided to take her underling with her? Noooo. That's too much to ask for. After all, I only did every little thing she asked of me, including keeping her damn secrets. Did y'all know she was the hit and run driver that killed Lucia? If only she could have killed Isabella too." Heather hocks a loogie, aiming it at Bella but missing by a long shot.

A second later there's a loud bang at the front of the house. We all crane our necks, trying to figure out what the hell has happened now. Before long, a team of heavily armed police officers and FBI agents descend into the kitchen.

"Looks like your time is up, Heather." Bella snickers. "You're going down after that beautiful confession you just delivered."

"I have no idea what you're talking about. I haven't said a word this entire time, and you can't prove otherwise."

The entire room goes silent. This crazy woman is trying to pass off her ranting as nothing more than a figment of our imaginations!

"Ma'am? Ma'am? Are you still there?" A woman's voice breaks through the silence, everyone turning to look at where the stranger's voice is coming from. "Ma'am? Ma'am, this is the 9-1-1 dispatcher you called about the home invasion."

Bella's confused face turns into one of recognition as she brings her smartwatch to her mouth, "Yes! I'm still here. I'm so sorry. I forgot I called you from my watch."

"Oh, don't worry. I just wanted to let you know that it's our protocol to record all incoming calls. This entire conversation has been recorded and can be pulled up for future review, if you'd so wish."

"Well, shit," Heather mumbles under her breath as the entire room breaks out into a combination of snickers or outright laughter.

Looks like there will be some justice after all.

Looking at Aiden's face, I can't say that William and Bella will be spared.

That guiser is about to blow, and there's no stopping what's to come.

ACTS OF GRACE

Chapter Twenty-Four

ASHLEY

My mouth refuses to cooperate as I take in everything Titus just told me. I mean, I knew Heather was tangled up with my mother, but holy hell.

Letting out a sound of disgust, I wrap my arms around Titus' broad shoulders. "That fucking bitch. She's lucky nothing happened to you or I would've ripped her limb from limb."

Titus chuckles into my hair. "I just told you your mother was trying to clean out your brother's bank account and all you can focus on is Heather and her half-assed attempt to take on hostages? Come on, baby. Have you no faith in my skills?"

My tongue taps the exterior of my upper lip as one of my hands trails down Titus' rock-hard chest. "Oh, I'm very aware of your skills." I stroke his pec, my fingers seeking his nipple before flicking it with force. But that doesn't change the fact that you are human, and anything could happen. Look at Aiden."

He takes my face in his hands, his eyes bouncing back and forth between mine. "I would never let that happen, Ashley." His lips find mine, his tongue tracing the contours of my mouth. "Nothing could take me from you. Not even death."

I close my eyes, resting my head against his chest. He smells of comfort and strength. His signature scent of cinnamon and musk is one I would recognize anywhere, one that would haunt me for all eternity if this man were to ever leave.

The realization of how much I've grown to care for this man sends a violent shiver running through me.

"What's the matter, little treasure?" Titus' hands rub up and down my arms, trying to soothe the deep ache that only one thing can.

Security.

"I know that we agreed to keep our relationship casual…"

Titus' body tenses as he pulls me back, his eyes boring into mine. "Talk to me, Ashley. Are you no longer happy with our arrangement?"

Arrangement.

The word sends my stomach roiling, making me want to hurl.

"An *arrangement* is what I had with Brad." I blow out a frustrated breath, rolling my eyes. "Without sounding cliche, I want to ask you something. But please be honest. I'm a big girl and I can take it. Whatever your answer might be."

Titus' lips roll in, biting back a smirk. "Okay, go on with it."

"After everything we've been through... do you really see what we have as being an arrangement? Is that all we are to you?"

Titus raises a brow, his lips pursing to the side. "We've declared our love for one another, and I've even claimed you." His fingers trace the outline of where my discreet collar rests. "I'd say our actions speak to us being more than a mere arrangement. We're tethered for life and thereafter."

My body melts into him, soaking up the love he's giving me in this moment. But that's the problem, it's just in this moment.

"I get what you're saying, Titus. But is that enough? Is it enough to live in the stolen moments, never once allowing ourselves to be public with our affection?" My eyes search his, trying to understand if he feels the same. "I'm like a wilting flower, starving for the sun's warmth, only to receive it under the darkness of clouds."

"What are you saying, *min skatt*? That you'll wither and die without a public declaration? Do my actions not speak of loyalty and love?" His brows are pushed together, his face marred with pain and confusion.

Talking to him is like talking to a brick wall. He doesn't understand, and I'm not sure he ever will.

Feeling defeated, I try to pull myself from his arms, but Titus isn't having it. "Answer me, woman." His growl is all business, but the concern in his eyes is clear.

My chest vibrates as my fingers dig into his flesh—frustration reaching its boiling point, having nowhere to go but out. "You want me to answer? Fine! There will come a time where it won't be enough. I am a woman, Titus. A woman who wants a family and a home. Something I never had growing up. The only good thing my parents did was have more than one child. I would've been lost without William." Titus hands drop from my side, his eyes widening as if frightened by a wild creature. "For heaven's sake, I was willing to give up on the idea of love just to hold some semblance of security with the likes of Brad Dawson. So to answer your question... It is enough for now, but that won't always be the case."

Titus blinks rapidly, "Are you giving me an ultimatum? Declare us publicly or lose you?"

"I guess I am." I take in a deep breath, knowing that the words I've just spoken have altered the future. A future that may not include Titus.

But the real question is, do I regret them?

ACTS OF GRACE

Chapter Twenty-Five

ASHLEY

PART II: *five months later...*

I'm grinning like a fool as I open the door to Bella and Cassie. It's our weekly girls' night, and I've been looking forward to this since Monday.

Things have been tense ever since I gave Titus my ultimatum. He never outright answered me, and I never brought it back up after the fact.

So far, we've been acting like it never happened, but I know it did. And the truth is, nothing's changed.

I'm still the same woman who wants a family—a home.

For the moment, though, I've been trying to live in every little bubble of bliss we have, cherishing the affection and laughter that the privacy these four walls provide.

If these walls could talk, they'd speak of stolen moments and lust filled nights, full of love and laughter.

Despite the awkward moment when I broke down and told him how I really felt, there hasn't been a night he hasn't been with me. Drama or not, the man hasn't left my side.

"What's up with you?" Cassie smirks as she walks past me and plops down on the white linen couch.

"Oh, we know what's up with her. I bet it starts with a T and ends with an S." Bella heads to my bar, grabbing the ice buckets, placing a bottle of white in one and sparkling water in another.

I still can't believe she's pregnant. I mean, I can. The way her and my brother are always on top of each other.

Another pang of jealousy hits, the need to have the same thing leaving an ache in my chest.

"Remind me why we have girls' nights, again? Seems like we're always talking about my non-relationship with Titus." I chuckle as I close the door behind me. "Instead we should be planning all of the upcoming nuptials. I swear, there must be something in the water. Babies and rings for everyone!"

Everyone except me.

"Um, nope. It's more like you're always avoiding the topic of your non-relationship with Titus. And as for wedding plans, Cassie's got it all covered, so how about we get back to you and Titus."

I put the tray of mixed nuts, olives, and various cheese on the island. "You know the drill ladies, help yourselves." Setting out the plates and napkins, I fully avoid the topic of Titus for the fifty-millionth time.

Yes, he's been staying here, and yes, we've been getting closer, but I've yet to stay the night at his home and he's yet to

230

come out and officially announce that we're together.

The situation is messy and I'm afraid that if I say anything, it will only rock the boat and end the cloud of bliss I'm on.

Bella pulls the sparkling water out of the bucket, her massive engagement ring glittering as she pours the bubbling contents into a cocktail glass. "Don't think you can ignore us forever. You'll have to talk about it eventually. It isn't healthy to bottle it all up inside. Trust me, I tried to do that when William had his hair brain scheme to incriminate Heather, and it almost cost us our relationship." She joins Cassie on the couch, the pregnancy glow only enhancing her natural beauty. "The past couple of months have definitely been a whirlwind of drama and chaos. I'm just glad everything has started to settle down."

Cassie snorts, popping an olive into her mouth. "You can say that again."

They aren't kidding. I've been living in my bubble of bliss with Titus but that hasn't stopped the world around us from spinning.

William finally divorced Heather after the truth came out about her connection to our mother and the bribing of the judges.

As soon as the decree was signed, William planned a getaway for him and Bella where he proposed. It was the most beautiful setting, held at a private beach on the cape.

Not long after, Ren and Cassie had their own share of drama, ending in their engagement and moving in together. Their new home is absolutely stunning, set along White Rock Lake with the most amazing view from almost every massive window in their million-dollar ranch style home.

There's a knock at the door, breaking me from my thoughts. "Yes, it's definitely been a crazy couple of months. With you two engaged, I think the next one in line is Charlotte." I pull the door open and let the lady in question step in.

"Did I hear my name?" Charlotte, Aiden's girlfriend comes bearing gifts. "Had to make a stop at the *chocolaterie* around the corner. They have the most amazing truffles, and I knew you ladies would appreciate them."

"I know I will!" Alyssa steps in from behind Charlotte, her long red hair swaying as she grabs a box for herself.

"Hey, those are for sharing." Charlotte admonishes, but the smile never leaves her face.

We've all sort of adopted Alyssa into the fold, like our baby sister. She's the youngest, only being seventeen.

Looking around the room, I can't help but smile. These ladies have become family, the sisters I always wished for growing up.

We all bring something different to the table and our small group of five wouldn't be what it is without a single one of them bringing their crazy selves to the mix.

"So, what's on the table today." Alyssa pops a truffle into her mouth as she plops down in another egg chair.

"Harassing Ashley into admitting there's something going on between her and Titus." Cassie snickers into her drink.

"I thought we already did that at Bella's. Didn't we all agree she should withhold the cookie until he publicly declares their relationship?" Alyssa waggles her brows before reaching for a glass and pouring herself some of the white.

Rolling my eyes, I finally join the others, sitting next to Cassie on the couch and reaching for my glass. "Enough with me and Titus. I gave him an ultimatum and he is yet to decide. Eventually it will be time to let him go, so how about we ignore that shit for now and let me be blissfully ignorant that my future could look like that of a sixty-year-old cat lady."

Looks of pity and outrage surround me and all I want to do is bury myself under towers of bon-bons, cheese, and wine.

"Oh, hunny. He will come to his senses." Charlotte sits to the other side of me, placing her hand on mine. "That man adores you, and even though he hasn't admitted it to the rest of us yet, it's as clear as day whenever he's around you. He looks at you as if you're his moon and stars."

"Then why is it so hard for him to come out and admit it to the others?" I know I sound like a petulant child, but I can't help it. I love the man so much and if he asked me to do anything for him, there'd be no hesitation.

"Who knows why men do anything. They call us complicated creatures when it's really them who do things ass-backward." Alyssa huffs out, blowing a crimson strand of hair from her face.

We all turn to look at the newest addition to our crew with raised brows all around. "Has our little baby found a boy she's interested in?" Bella squeaks as she claps her hands together.

Alyssa laughs out loud, "Baby? Last I checked you were only one year older than me!"

"Two. I'm nineteen now." Bella scowls while the rest of us chuckle.

"So, is Bella right?" I ask, partly curious, partly trying to lift the heat from the whole Titus conversation.

Alyssa sighs, "Sort of. It doesn't matter anyway. Nothing could ever come of it and based on how he acts around me, I think I'm more of a nuisance to him than a possible love interest."

"*Nuisance.* That's an interesting word choice…" Charlotte purses her lips as she eyes the rest of us.

We all know that Hudson's father asked him to host his stepsister while she went to college in Dallas. From what we understand, it wasn't really a favor but more of a demand.

"Yes. Nuisance. Like I said, I doubt anything will come of it. Anyway, now that everything's settled down—Heather and Marissa both being in prison— we should all plan a trip together. WRATH lockdown was no joke and I appreciate the freedoms Hudson has *allowed.*" Alyssa pops another truffle into her mouth with another roll of her eyes.

"Freedom." I scoff at the complete misuse of the word. "I don't think we could ever be truly free while being ladies of WRATH."

"This is true, but hey, at least we aren't those judges who helped Marissa and heather out." Cassie shrugs her shoulders and winces. "God, I heard they were stripped of their titles, publicly reprimanded and are currently on trial with all of their assets seized."

"Yes, one of them even committed suicide!" Bella blurts out while bringing a hand to her chest.

I take a sip of my drink, not feeling sorry for any of them. Not even my own mother. "They all knew what they were doing. If they didn't like the idea of being dressed in orange, they should've considered that possibility before they all joined forces in an effort to destroy lives."

The girls all nod in unison, the comfortable quiet creating a solemn mood. Needing to break us out of this darkness, I bring my hands together with a loud smack. "Okay, enough of the doom and gloom." I grab the remote and turn on the T.V. "How about we watch *Kill for Me,* the new movie adaptation for V. Domino's Dark Renzetti series.

"Yessss. Love me some Nico." Cassie lets out a low whistle as she rubs her hands together.

"Now that's some doom and gloom I can get behind any day." Charlotte chimes in. "Nico might be a psychopath, but he's my psychopath."

"Oh no, I call dibs." I playfully growl before hitting play.

I'm joking… *but not really.*

Nico 'the cold' Renzetti is mine.

Chapter Twenty-Six

A shley is passed out on the couch, remote still in her hand. The girls left about fifteen minutes ago, and I doubt they stirred to wake her.

I'm about to turn the television off when I see what's playing, *Kill for Me.*

I chuckle, wondering if these ladies know that this movie is based on the real life Renzetti brothers, the notorious Famiglia based out of New York.

Ashley stirs as I lift her, mumbling something that has my blood thumping in my ears, "Nico is mine, bitches. I called dibs."

She did not just say that.

My knees hit the foot of the bed as I lower her onto the mattress, my hand twitching and ready for a spanking.

"Titus? When did you get home?" Her eyes are squinting, trying to adjust to the dim light of the room. "Are the girls still here?"

"I got in a couple of minutes ago. No, the girls are gone. And no, you cannot and will not have Nico."

Ashley's eyes shoot wide open, her brows reaching toward her hairline. "What? What are you talking about?"

"I'm talking about you calling dibs on Nico. You do know he's an actual person, right? An actual person with a murderous wife who will no doubt slice your tongue out for saying her man is yours."

Her face puckers, eyes narrowing with rage. "Were you spying on our girls' night!?"

"No. You mumbled it in your sleep, and nice to know you're talking about your fantasies with another man while I'm away from home."

"I didn't know he was real. But could you really blame me for fantasizing about having a relationship with a man who loves his woman so much he's willing to kill for her, let alone be with her publicly as his partner."

I take a step back, feeling as if I've been stabbed in the heart. How the fuck could she think I don't love her like that? Is that how little she thinks of me?

My jaw ticks and my breathing deepens.

"If my actions haven't proven to you that my love for you is true, that I *would* kill for you, that you are my fucking world— then I've been wasting my time."

With a shake of my head, I turn to walk out of the room I've been sharing with my beautifully stubborn woman. Not one night has gone by where I've left her side. Sure, I could've brought her to my home—a home I've shared with others—but it never felt right. This tiny one-bedroom apartment felt more like home than my massive estate ever did.

Well, it did *up until today.*

"Titus!" Ashley shouts, stopping me from reaching for the door. "Where are you going?"

"Home, because this isn't it." My heart cracks open, watching the pain etch on Ashley's face. *Did I put it there?* I think we both did. "My woman would never question my love, my loyalty. Over what? A fucking title?"

Her mouth hangs open, her beautiful lips begging me to come kiss the pain away, but I can't.

Not now that I know how she truly feels.

"Titus." My name is but a whisper on her lips while her eyes plead for me to stay. "It's not just a title. It's what it means. The safety and security, the permanence it brings."

"Permanence? What does that even mean? Please enlighten me, because in my opinion, a title doesn't mean shit. People get married and divorced all the fucking time. What did that title do for them? Jack shit."

Ashley blinks repeatedly, silent tears falling down her face, shattering what little was left of my heart and decimating it into oblivion.

"I guess it doesn't. Not if the people who give it don't mean what the title implies." She kneels on the bed, a hand wiping away her tears. "But that's never what I asked for, that's not something I'd ever want."

Frustrated at her words, I stalk toward her, grabbing her shoulders before dropping my hands from her sides. "Then what do you want, *min skatt?* I'm not psychic."

Her brows push together, eyes narrowing into thin slits. "I'm not asking you to be psychic, Titus. All I ever wanted was to be public about what we share. Not have to deny shit to my friends and family. I want you to be proud of having me by your side. Instead, you choose to wait around until the girls have left the apartment in order to come up and slip into my bed."

I scoff, irritated at the fact that she can't see this is all for her. "I do this to keep you safe, so that your relationship with your brother isn't strained. You think I enjoy having to watch what I say around him? I'm constantly having to keep Hudson in check who's already slipped up more than once." My hand runs through my hair, tugging at it, about to pull it out in frustration. "He'd never be okay with you and me, Ashley. I know the moment I come clean, all hell will break loose."

"But why? He, of all people, has no leg to stand on. He's with his best friend's niece and his friend's daughter. It doesn't get more off-limits than that."

I huff, "It's not about what I am to him, but what I am as a person."

"What?" Ashley's face scrunches up in confusion as her arms reach toward me, her delicate hands intertwining behind my neck and pulling me to her. "What are you talking about?"

Without hesitation, I follow, lowering her onto the bed as my body crawls over hers. "I'm a monster. The creature that goes bump in the night. No respectable brother would ever let his sister near me, let alone in my bed."

Ashley licks her lips as her legs wrap around my waist. "You, Titus Bonde, are no monster. You are my knight—the rock I lean upon when the world is too much."

I smile, letting the warmth that her words bring soothe my broken heart. "You have to remember, *min skatt*, your brother has seen me at my worst. He and the other men of WRATH were the ones to save me from myself." Rocking myself against her, I trail my nose along the length of her jaw before placing a kiss on her chin. "Were it not for them, I would've continued on the path of self-destruction. I still have my darkness, but now, I use it for good instead of evil."

Ashley nips at my jaw, her fingers scraping the scruff along my face. "Seems to me like this monster is more of an angel."

I chuckle, unable to hold back the laughter. "Oh, little treasure, I'm definitely no angel." My fingers slide her dress up before dipping under the hem of her panties and finding that sweet heaven I love so much. "Only a sinner would revel in lighting up your body like this." Stroking between her folds, I let my fingers play in her juices, enjoying the delicious sounds she makes.

Yes. I'm *definitely* a sinner.

Chapter Twenty-Seven

ASHLEY

Walking through the threshold of William's home, I ask myself what the hell I'm doing.

All morning I've been at war with myself. *Should I come clean with William or should I leave it up to Titus?*

Titus made it clear that the only thing holding him back was my brother and how it would affect my relationship with him. He's not even worried about his relationship with the men of WRATH which speaks volumes.

The fact that he's willing to forgo a relationship with William, or his other friends for that matter, all for me is beyond what any declaration of love could mean.

The least I could do is bear the brunt of this argument with

William for us—for our future.

I know William will be mad at first, but like I told Titus, he's got no leg to stand on.

"Hey! What are you doing here?" William's smile meets my hesitant one, and I know it's now or never.

"Hey..." I close his office door behind me and take a seat on the leather armchair in front of his massive oak desk.

"Uh-oh. I know that look. What did you do?" William raises a brow, his lips smirking.

"Um, why does it necessarily have to be me who did something?" I try to sound offended, but I know that I did in fact do something and that he probably won't be too happy with that something.

"Come on. We grew up together, I know all of your tells. Now talk, what's going on and do I have to kick someone's ass?"

I visibly flinch at his words. I pray to God that this doesn't end in his trying to kick someone's ass. "Before we talk, I want to know how things are between you and Bella. I know I gave you a hard time in the beginning, but it was never because I didn't like her or want her as part of our family. It was because of our father's secrets and what I thought it would do to her when she found out."

William's brows push together, concern visibly growing on his face. "Of course, I know that. You two seem to be getting on as thick as thieves. And we're doing great. I can't wait to grow our family and I'm already trying to pressure her for a third baby." His face goes from a frown to a huge grin and then back to a frown, all in the span of a minute. "But what does all that have to do with what you want to talk to me about?"

The room grows quiet, the sound of my swallowing filling the void and making William's visible concern grow. "I bring it up because I don't want you to think that the fact that Bella is over a decade younger, your best friend's niece, or your friend's daughter is something that I'd ever look down upon."

Understanding reaches his eyes, his jaw ticking and fist clenching beating clear indicators that he knows what I'm getting at. "Who? Who is it, Ashley? Which one of my brothers has crossed the line?"

My mouth goes dry and my lips suddenly lose their ability to work.

"Ashley, tell me now or so help me god..."

"What? What will you do, William? Give them shit for something you're guilty of doing yourself? That's a bit of the pot calling the kettle black, isn't it?"

William sneers, his knuckles cracking as he flexes his hands. "It all depends, dear sister. You don't know these men like I do. Some of them, they're too damaged. They could never give you what you need."

"So, what you're saying is that you see yourself as better than some of your so-called brothers. Because last I checked, you and I have our own set of baggage and from what I've seen, you've still gone forward and robbed the cradle." My stomach churns, knowing that I've just dealt a low blow, but I couldn't help it— he's being a hypocrite.

William closes his eyes, taking in a deep breath. "Just tell me one thing, sister. Tell me it isn't Titus."

My mouth drops open, unable to answer. Of all the names he could have picked, his go-to was the man I love.

William's fist pounds the desk, "Damn it, Ashley. Why him? Of all the men in the world, why him?"

Fury boils within me, heating me to my core and making me act before thinking. Standing up, I slam both of my palms onto his desk, "Why not him?! He's always been there for me. In my darkest moments, it has always been him who've I leaned on. The knight who rescues me from my nightmares and delivers me into bliss."

William's face puckers, a visible tint of green tinging his skin. "Do not talk to me about bliss with Titus." William gets up from his desk and walks over to his bar before pouring himself a healthy pour of whiskey. "Look, I'm going to give it to you straight. You're a woman and I'm not going to talk to you through rose colored glasses. Titus, I love him like a brother, but he has issues. I'm not sure he's capable of having what it takes to be a good partner."

My eyes narrow, taking offense at his words. "You're not the one who lies in bed with him at night. You're not the one he comforts. You're not the one he protects, leaving his needs last in order to ensure yours are met." I walk over to him, grabbing the tumbler from his hand and taking it for myself. "I am. I'm that person. I've been that person and I can tell you from experience, he has what it takes."

I take a massive gulp from the glass, the amber liquid burning on its way down. Even though I've just declared myself to my brother, there's still a part of me that thinks William might be right, that Titus might not want to be the kind of partner I need. *A husband. A father.*

William pours himself another glass before going back to his desk, this time sitting on top of the wooden piece.

"Ashley, I'm not sure you know everything there is to know about him. If you did, I don't think you'd be coming in here all gung-ho ready to fight me to the death over this."

I throw my head back, letting out a deep sigh. "Titus told me he sees himself as a monster. That you'd see him as one too."

Lifting my head, my gaze meets William's, "I can tell you right now, there is nothing you can tell me that will make me stop loving that man."

William sucks in a sharp breath, "So it's like that, is it?"

I give him a small nod. "It's like that."

"Well, I'm still your brother and that means that I have a duty to protect you. That duty extends above and beyond whatever loyalty I owe my friends." William throws back the contents of his glass, grimacing as he hisses. "I'm going to tell you what I know of Titus—what I've seen. If you still want to be with him after that, then don't say I didn't warn you."

It's my turn to throw back the contents of my drink, slamming the tumbler onto the desk once I'm done. "Like I said, nothing could make me stop loving him."

"Since you're in love with him, and you've implied he's been in your *bed*," William's face contorts, his throat bobbing as he swallows audibly, "I assume you know the kind of kink he's into."

My face heats and I'm unable to look my brother in the eye. "Yes."

One word. That's all I can muster. This is already awkward as hell, and I'm not about to go into the details of my sex life with one of his best friends.

"Okay, well, he's always been like that. Liked that type of stuff." William closes his eyes and mumbles, "I can't believe I'm talking to you about this shit."

"I can't either, as far as I'm concerned, what we do in our bed is none of your business."

William's eyes shoot open, his hardened gaze staring me down. "It very damn well *is* my business if it can end up killing you."

My brows push together, my head tilting to the side. "What are you talking about? Sure, he likes it a little rough, but he's never once put me in danger."

Blowing out a breath, William crouches down, his hands reaching for mine. "Look, what I'm about to tell you will be upsetting so just hear me out til' the end."

"Okay." I give him a hesitant nod, unsure of what could be so scary.

"Remember how in high school we used to have parties at Hudson's house? His parents were never home, and he had no siblings who would rat him out, so it was the perfect spot to do whatever the fuck we wanted and not get in trouble."

"Yes, I remember. You used to think you were so slick, sneaking off in the middle of the night. As if we didn't know where you were heading." I smile, my thoughts going back to simpler times.

"Okay, well, on one of those nights we had a huge party. It was late into the night and mostly everyone had cleared out except for the crew and a couple of drunk stragglers. I was out back by the pool with Hudson and Ren, recapping our adventures for the night when all of a sudden a panicked and half-dressed Titus comes rushing at us. I'll never forget what he said or what we saw next."

My hands squeeze William's, "Just spit it out."

William looks away, unable to meet my gaze as he delivers the words that rock me to my core. "He was freaking out, mumbling, 'I killed her. I fucking killed her.' over and over again."

My mouth hangs open, trying to digest the scene he's just described.

"In that moment we thought all was lost. No matter what,

we'd stand by him because he was one of us. Our brother. But in that moment, we didn't know what to do. So, we just followed him. Followed him right into a back bedroom where this girl lay naked and passed out. She had her legs bound, her arms tied above her head, mouth gagged, and her neck... there was a belt around it."

My hand reaches up to my mouth as I gasp for air, this revelation making things so much clearer when it comes to my tortured man.

William places his hand on my shoulder and squeezes, "We all did what we could. We tried to save the girl. But it was too late. She was gone."

"No," my face contorts as I try to make sense of everything I've just learned. Yes, Titus likes things rough, but he's always been so careful. "This can't be true."

I push away from William, getting up from my chair and toppling it over.

"Ashley, wait, there's more. You have to listen."

"No. This isn't real. This is all a lie. You're telling me this so I won't want to be with Titus anymore. That's all this is." I rush to the door, needing to escape my brother's words. Words that have dug deep into my heart, creating a growing wound that won't stop bleeding.

How could the man I love keep such a massive secret from me?

This *can't* be true, for if it is, then I'm in love with a monster.

Chapter Twenty-Eight

TITUS

"No, Ashley isn't with me. Why are you asking, and have you checked with her detail?" William sounds equal parts panicked and pissed off, the lethal combination having my hackles rising.

"Yes, I've checked with her detail. I wouldn't be asking you otherwise." He spits out, the fury in his tone palpable through the receiver.

"You mean to tell me her detail lost track of her?!" It's my turn to snarl. William can be pissed all he wants, but Ashley's safety takes precedence. "Where the fuck do we hire these men, Rent-A-Cop? How in the hell have we managed to be number one in the nation when we can't even keep track of one woman?"

William hisses into the phone, his breathing loud and fast. "This wouldn't be a problem if it weren't for your inability to keep your cock in your pants."

"Excuse me? What did you just say?" The world stops and my breathing goes right along with it.

Did he find out about us? What does this have to do with Ashley's security team?

"You heard me. If you just would've kept your dick in your pants, we wouldn't be having this conversation. Ashley would've never fallen in love with you, I never would have had to have told her the truth about you, and she never would've stormed out of my home like a bat out of hell, losing the fucking crew that was watching her."

All of his words hit me at once, rolling around my head and making it difficult to breathe.

Despite the chaos taking over my brain, one thing sticks out louder than a two-year-old throwing a tantrum.

Ashley is missing.

She's fucking missing.

"What, you've got nothing to say for yourself? How convenient." William sneers, the sarcasm oozing from his voice.

"If you have something to say, say it." I've had enough of his insinuations, there's much more important shit at hand than playing the blame game.

"Why? Why did you have to go after my sister? After everything we've been through, you chose someone who was off-limits."

I scoff, unable to believe my ears. "That's rich, coming from you. Aren't you best friends with Ren, Bella's uncle? Oh, and isn't Bella's father one of our good friends too?"

William growls, his words coming out slow and deliberate.

"I'm. No. Killer."

I bellow out in laughter, unable to hold back from the utmost idiotic comment I've ever heard. "First, we're in the business of killing, brother. You may not have done any killing with your own hands, but it's part and parcel of what we do in the business. To wash your hands of what our duties may call for is absolutely blind or willfully ignorant." I hear him begin to speak, but I'm not done. "Second, you damn well know I didn't kill that girl. I *knew* you'd try and use that against me. I tried to warn Ashley."

"Well, you clearly didn't because the way she walked out of here she looked as if she'd lost her damn mind."

My breathing picks up and my jaw clenches, "I should have been the one to tell her about that, William."

He laughs sardonically, "You cannot be giving me shit right now. You fuck my sister, drag her into your perverted-ass-ways, ways that could end her life, and you dare give *me* shit?"

"I didn't kill her!" I roar into the line, needing to remind myself of the truth just as much as he does. "She was all drugged out and died from an overdose... I didn't know." My fist slams into the wall, my knuckles cracking as they bust through the drywall.

"Are you sure about that, Titus? Are you one hundred percent sure you didn't choke her to death?"

The fateful night keeps looping over and over again in my head. *The lanky blond laying on the mattress, her lips tinged blue and her lifeless eyes staring blankly at the ceiling.*

Closing my eyes, I take in a centering breath. I. Did. Not. Kill. Her.

My hand reaches down, touching her face but there's no response. She's no longer here. She's gone.

The coroner report said she died from a heart attack induced by the drugs in her system. I. Did. Not. Kill. Her.

"Are you sure you want to try this?" I ask the blonde, needing to make sure she isn't going to freak out halfway.

"Yes. I'll do whatever, be whatever, and want whatever you want. So long as I get to tell the girls I bagged myself the T." She lolls her head to side as she giggles, meanwhile I roll my eyes.

At school, our crew is known as WRATH. Each girl trying to make the rounds and bag every member in order to spell out the word WRATH, as if we were some sort of Pokémon card.

Whatever. At least I know it means she'll be willing to try something new with me.

My hands shake as I tie her up the way I've learned, keeping her on all fours the entire time.

Once I'm done, I add the finishing touch. Adding a collar and clipping on a leash I grab her by the neck, laying her back onto the bed with the use of my hand alone.

I'm about to unzip my pants and make her suck me off when I see it. Her face. It's devoid of any emotion. Not a shred of light to be found in those soulless eyes.

Fuck. Fuck. Fuuuuuck.

I try and shake her awake, but there is no response.

She's as limp as a rag doll and her lips have already turned blue.

I know I was rough when I grabbed her by the neck, but surely that move alone couldn't have done this...could it?

Not knowing what to do, I go find my new friends. One of them must know CPR or some shit. Maybe we can bring her back.

We have to bring her back.

"Titus!" William yells before mumbling, "Fucking hell. Titus! Are you there?"

"Yes, I'm here and I didn't fucking kill her. But you knew that

254

already."

"I did." I hear him sigh through the line, the rustling of fabric and the slamming of a car door playing in the background. "But unfortunately for Ashley, I didn't get to that part."

My blood turns into ice. "What do you mean, William?"

"I mean, I was having a heart to heart with my sister when she stormed out and didn't let me finish explaining about you." He blows out a breath before continuing. "I told her about you killing that girl, but I didn't clarify that she may have also died from a drug overdose."

I growl, "There is no maybe. The coroner said she died from a drug induced heart attack! How the fuck does that equate to me killing her?"

"You very well could have killed her with that asphyxiation kink of yours. At the very least you could've saved her if you weren't too damn busy tying her up."

My chest burns, feeling as if I'd just had a dagger rip it wide open. There it is, the truth of the matter.

I *am* a monster.

I *could* have saved her.

But I didn't. Instead, I was so focused on my desire that I completely ignored the woman under my care.

I failed her.

Maybe William is right. I know I definitely don't deserve Ashley, and I've lost myself so many times in her that it's possible I could hurt that which I love the most.

William's harsh voice cuts through my mental flogging, "We can talk about this later. Right now we need to search for my sister. I'll assemble a new team. Meanwhile, we can all divide and search for her at the spots she frequents."

"On it." I end the call, not waiting for further instruction.

I don't need to listen to him reprimand me or give me orders. If anyone knows where my little treasure will be, it's me.

She's my everything and there is no other man on this earth that would seek her out the way I can and will.

Ashley Hawthorne will be located and returned to safety, free from all harm.

That includes me.

I am a monster, and as much as I hate to admit it, William is right. Who's to say that I won't lose control with Ashley and hurt her in my lust induced fog?

As much as it pains me, I think it's time I let her go.

ACTS OF GRACE

Chapter
Twenty-Nine
ASHLEY

My body shakes as I try to process my brother's words. The ice-cold drizzle of rain pelts my face as I gain my bearings, the water soaking my clothes and making it stick to me like a second skin.

I stormed out of William's home without my bag or clue of where in the hell I was going.

I'm in an alley, not sure how I got here.

These old neighborhoods are all connected by little alleys, intertwining the massive lots and keeping the garbage hidden out back.

Quite literally. Rows of trash cans line the narrow path as I try to navigate my way back home.

Titus killed a submissive.

Titus *killed* a submissive.

The words keep looping in my head over and over again.

So much makes sense now.

The way he hesitates at certain points in our play.

He has to know that I'd tell him if I thought he was really hurting me, right?

Gah, I need to find him. I have so many questions and I need answers.

The screeching of tires has me whirling around, just in time to see a black SUV come to a halt, and a face I know all too well stepping out.

"Brad? What are you doing here?" I blink repeatedly, trying to make sure this isn't some sort of dream.

"You're one tough broad to get alone. You always have those men lurking, keeping me away." He sneers as he paces toward me.

"You've been trying to reach me?" My brows push together, confused as hell because I haven't gotten a call from him in months.

Definitely not since the run-in at the bar.

"Yes and no." I tilt my head, inspecting the man I dedicated over a year of my life to. He's dressed just as I remember, only everything seems to look out of place.

His shirt is wrinkled, as if he's slept in it, and there are dark circles under his eyes. "Brad, are you okay? You look... different."

"Questions, questions, questions. Enough with the fucking questions."

His tone catches me off-guard. I definitely wasn't expecting attitude and I definitely wasn't expecting him to lunge at me like he just did.

"Motherfucker," I mutter as I narrowly escape his grasp and take off at full speed.

"Get back here you little bitch!" Brad runs after me, his hand reaching out and pulling me back by my hair.

My whole body jerks back, feet lifting off the ground as I slam back into Brad. "Let me go, you cheating asshole."

I throw my elbow back, getting him good in the gut.

"You're going to pay for that." Brad yanks my hair once more, bringing his mouth to my ear. "I should've ended you when I had the chance."

My body goes rigid at his words. "Look, Brad, I think we can both agree we weren't a good match. So—"

"Quiet. I've listened to your annoying voice long enough." He starts to walk us back toward the SUV and I know that if I want to remain alive, I need to avoid getting in that car at all costs.

I'm still able to move a little, even though he's got his hand dug into the back of my head, keeping me somewhat subdued.

Refusing to go out without a fight, I throw everything I have into elbowing him before whipping around and kneeing him in the nose. Blood begins to gush from his face, letting me know that's my cue to leave.

"Oh no you don't." Brad wraps his arms around my waist and hoists me over his shoulder, carrying me off to the back of the SUV.

I'm about to start shouting for help when I feel the sting of a prick on my thigh.

What the fuck?

"Goodnight, little whore." Are the last words I hear as the world I love fades to black.

"Wake up, I want you to see what you've done to yourself."
Brad's voice pulls me from deep sleep.

Cracking my eyes open, I see he's taken me to suicide bridge
as the locals have dubbed it.

Oh, hell no.

I try to fight, move in any way, but I can't. It's as if my arms
and legs were stuck in a vat of cement.

Every part of me feels heavy, unable to move.

Brad sneers, "You dumb bitch. You think I'd risk you getting
up and running away? You're nice and drugged up, there's no
way you're walking out of this alive."

My stomach flips at the realization that he's probably right.
"Why?" I mumble through the gag he's placed around my
mouth.

"You really are dumb, aren't you? My name is Brad *Dawson.*
You know, as in the Honorable Andrew Dawson's son." He rolls
his eyes, annoyed at the fact that I hadn't connected the dots on
my own.

My eyes widen as I try and sputter incoherent words. How
had I missed that? It must've been the shock in combination with
the fact that mother was after William and his money, not me.

Brad sees the confusion on my face and laughs sardonically.
"I cannot believe you could be this dumb."

I growl, trying to head butt him with as much energy I can
muster.

I had a lot of things going on, not to mention that the

discovery of my mother being alive had thrown me for a loop all on its own.

I don't care what this jackass says, I'm *not* dumb, and this will *not* be my end.

My eyes flicker back and forth down the lonely bridge and I try and decipher what time it is. Is it even the same day? How long have I been out?

Brad is busy placing a piece of paper under a rock, it's crumpled and looks to be in my own handwriting.

What the—? Motherfucker. He's going to try to stage my suicide!

The only thing I have left is my voice, since my limbs aren't going to be helping me at the moment.

I'll try and talk to him, and if that fails... I yell.

"Why, Brad?" The gargled words soak the cloth placed around my mouth making me want to gag.

"Why?" He chuckles, his eyes sparkling with dark intent. "You ruined the only chance I had with my father. That's why."

My brows push together, unsure of what his father being guilty of a crime has anything to do with him.

"Ugh. I'll have to spell everything out for you, won't I?" He sighs, leaning his frame against the railing. "I was a bastard child. The only reason why I carry my father's name is because my mother ensured it, despite my father's wishes. Like any shunned child, I wanted to earn the love I so desperately lacked. That meant I did anything and everything I could to earn my father's affection. Finally, I'd achieved what I wanted. I got his attention when I graduated top of my class and passed the Florida Bar exam."

Brad pushes himself off of the railing and begins to pace in front of me, all while glaring. "He said I could earn a spot on the yearly family retreat if I helped his mistress out. I didn't think anything of it. He's my father and he'd finally paid attention to me. There's no way I'd let him down. All I had to do was gather intel on your brother and feed it back to Marissa."

He stops in front of me, gently stroking my hair before yanking it and my head along with it. "Everything was going according to plan, up until you left. Then the men of WRATH made it damn near impossible to reach you." He releases my head from his grasp, flinging me back onto the floor, making me grunt. "And now... Now my father is dead. You and your little friends ruined him. He's dead because of you."

"But I left because you cheated." I mutter, somewhat inaudible, not even sure it really speaks to the point anymore. It's clear that I'm not going to be able to talk him out of whatever he has planned. His psychotic kidnapping stems from some deep-rooted abandonment issue.

"But the joke is on you. Turns out your end will be just like his." Brad storms toward me, lifting his foot and rearing it before kicking me in the ribs. "Welcome to your suicide you stupid bi—"

Mid-sentence, Brad stops, his eyes going wide before he stumbles back.

What in the world?

That's when I see it. The crimson color seeping through his crumpled dress shirt. *He's been shot!*

Self-preservation kicks in and I will my body with everything I have to roll. I need to get out of the shooter's line of site until I know if they're good or bad.

I pray that they're good.

I've managed to get myself face down when I hear the scuffle of footsteps running toward me.

Fuck. Fuck. Fuck.

Strong hands grip my arms from behind, lifting me and pressing my back to their chest.

It's now or never, Ashley.

Using the last bit of energy I have, I fling my head back, hearing that delicious crunch of bone and a not so delicious grunt from a voice I know too well.

"Ooof. *Min skatt*, it's me." Titus' pained voice groans behind me, letting me melt back into his arms.

Despite my possibly having broken his nose, I have no doubt in my mind that this man would never hurt me.

I am, and forever will be, his.

Chapter Thirty

I'm not sure that my telling her it's me is any sort of reassurance. Especially if she thinks I'm a killer.

Well, I am, but only when the job calls for it. Never of a woman under my care.

I look her over making sure there are no serious wounds, all while keeping an eye on the fucking asshole lying face up on the concrete.

I was able to get a couple of shots in with the silencer, enough to keep him down but not dead.

No. I'm not done with that prick and if he thinks the worst of his pathetic life was getting ignored by his father... well, let's just say he's about to find out there's a whole new world of pain out there, and it's all coming for him.

"Titus." Ashley looks up at me with the last thing I expect to see—love.

Fear, disgust, and maybe indifference. I expected any of these, but not love.

"Yes, little treasure."

"I love you." Her words are whispered, but I hear them.

I squeeze her body as I bring it to mine, wanting to absorb all of her into me, making us one. "I love you too. More than you could ever know."

Her eyes blink, looking deep into mine. "I know, because I feel it too."

A gargled voice breaks into our moment and right then I wish I would have gone in with an extra shot. "Awe, well isn't this fucking sweet." Brad coughs and sputters, choking on his own blood. "So now that you're re-united, what's your plan? Taking me to the hospital and then getting me locked up like you did my father?"

Laying Ashley gently on the ground, I rise, stalking toward this pathetic excuse of a man. "You'd like that, wouldn't you?"

His brows push together confused with my question. "What? Why would anyone in their right mind want to go to prison?"

I laugh, amazed at how clueless this man is. "You think that prison is the worst we can do to you? We are the men of WRATH, our connections spread far and wide. There isn't a method of torture we haven't seen, and not a one we wouldn't be willing to try on you."

Brad sputters before swallowing down whatever he just gurgled up. "But you can't. That's illegal."

My hand acts of its own accord, reaching out and grabbing his neck before squeezing until his eyes are practically bulging out of his head. "And was throwing Ashley off a bridge *legal?*"

"But, but... you're not me. You're the good guy."

I sneer, "Good guy, bad guy. Things aren't always black and white. All you need to know is that you've crossed a line, one that you could never come back from. As far as your fate? You'll have to wait and see. Lucky for you, I owe my brothers for having kept a secret."

Brad's face contorts, "How does that make me lucky?"

I slap him lightly on the face, "By offering you up to my brothers, you avoid the Titus Torture Special... Well, that is if they don't choose it as your punishment."

I hear Ashley snort behind me, and I'm glad she's finding amusement in Brad pissing his pants.

"You won't get away with this!" Brad squeaks.

"Watch me." I grin from ear to ear before cocking my fist and slamming it straight against his temple, knocking him the fuck out.

Turning back to Ashley, I offer a softer smile. "Okay, princess. Let's get you home."

Ashley

My eyes blink open, the dim lighting of my room sneaking through and making me realize I'm back home.

Alive and safe, thanks to Titus.

"You're awake." Titus lowers himself onto the side of the bed as he strokes my head.

"Yes. I mean, I feel like I'm stuck in quicksand still, but look,"

I lift up my hand and wiggle my fingers slowly.

Titus smiles, "Yes, the doctor said that you should have full faculty of your extremities within the next hour or so. Thankfully, that fucker didn't use enough drugs to cause permanent damage."

I cringe, knowing this could've been so much worse. "God, how did you find me?" Titus touches my neck, lifting the beautiful platinum collar he gifted me.

"There's a tracker in the pendant." He raises a brow when he sees the outrage on my face. "I never used it to check up on you and only had it as a fail-safe in case everything went to hell. Which it did. So, you're welcome."

This man has the audacity to smirk at me right now. "You're just lucky this all worked out. Had I found out about this beforehand, you would've been in big trouble."

His hand lingers on my chest, his fingers gently tracing an invisible line along my neck and making my heart sink.

I know where his thoughts are and the reason behind the storm in his eyes.

"Ash—"

"No, Titus. I need you to hear me out."

Titus gives me a solemn nod, his hand retracting from my body.

Taking his hand in mine, I return it to my chest, laying his palm flat over my heart. "Do you feel this, Titus? It's my heart, and it beats for you. There is nothing in this world that could ever make me stop loving you. You could slay a million souls and my heart would still be yours." I bring a hand to his face, my fingers tracing the contours of his chiseled mouth. "You're ingrained into every part of me and to remove you would be to split me in two. I would not survive it."

Titus goes to speak but I press my fingers over his lips. "Please, let me finish."

His glistening eyes blink, releasing a tear down the planes of his masculine face. Placing a soft kiss to my fingers, my man lets me continue. "I don't care what you've done in the past. All I know is that you are mine and I am yours. You would never do anything to harm me or those I love. I know this just as I know my heart will only ever beat for you."

Titus lets out a choked sob as he pulls me to him, squeezing me so tight I feel it in my bones. "Ashley, my little treasure. I don't deserve you. Even when you think I've killed, you still give yourself to me. Unconditionally, I know you are mine."

I pull back enough to look into his eyes, "Always, unconditionally."

A soft smile plays on my man's plump lips. "Well, it's good to know that you'd stand by me no matter what. But there's something you need to know... I didn't kill that girl."

My brows reach up to my hair line and my mouth opens into an 'O.' "What do you mean? But I thought..."

Brushing a loose strand from my face, Titus sighs. "William didn't finish telling you everything. The jerk led in with the worst of it but didn't get to tell you that the girl had died from an overdose of whatever cocktail she was on." He shakes his head and sucks in his lips, audibly breathing in and out before continuing. "That doesn't mean that I didn't have a role in her death. Instead of being so caught up in what I was doing, I could've been paying attention to the signs. I could've intervened sooner. Maybe she'd still be alive."

"Oh, Titus. You were just a kid back then. You reacted just as any other teenager your age would've." I feel my face transform from one of concern to one of fury. "I can't believe my damn brother skipped out on a vital piece of information."

"To his defense, he said you stormed out without giving him a chance to explain." Titus smirks.

He freaking smirks!

"I cannot believe you're sitting here, standing up for the man when he was trying to throw you under the bus!" I scoff, shaking my head from left to right.

"Hey, he was trying to protect his baby sister. I can't really blame him. And to be fair, I knew this was going to happen eventually. I'd just planned it all so differently."

Titus reaches for the nightstand where he keeps his things, pulling out a pair of socks and then a tiny black velvet box within them.

That sneaky bastard.

My hands fly up to my mouth as soon as my brain registers what he's holding.

Titus chuckles as he takes my hand in his, his body moving off the bed and kneeling right beside it. "This is definitely not how I planned it, but I can't see myself holding back one second longer."

Unbidden tears stream down my face at the sight before me. My man, my beautifully damaged and lethal man, kneeling on one knee. It's what I've always dreamt of, what I've always wanted, and now it's finally here.

"Ashley Hawthorne, my queen. I'm not good with words so excuse me as I speak from my heart. I may not be the most eloquent or sentimental man, but I do know one thing, and it's that I never want to spend a day without calling you mine." He reaches out, grabbing my hand while popping open the little black box.

I gasp, looking down at the impeccable cushion cut diamond set on a delicate platinum band. It's absolutely stunning.

"You may deserve a man that's a million times better than me, but I'm selfish. I knew you were off-limits. I knew I was too damaged and that you needed more. But I caved, letting myself taste you. And instead of searching for redemption or seeking atonement, I found my saving grace in you. You've freed me from the shackles of my past and shown me that the future is bright with you in it. You are a light, a beacon of hope, and I want you all for me. Now and forever, I want you to be mine. Mine to treasure. Mine to pleasure. Mine to adore."

Tears keep falling as I take in his words of devotion. "Titus Eirik Bonde, I'll follow you to the ends of this earth and beyond. I am now, and forever will be, yours. Yours to treasure. Yours to pleasure. Yours to adore."

Titus' hands shake as he slides on the beautiful ring, the physical embodiment of our love, and my heart soars. Nothing could ruin this moment. Absolutely nothing.

I wrap my arms around Titus' neck, bringing him to me when there's a loud pounding at the door.

"What the—" I mumble at the same time as my brother's voice booms into my apartment.

"Open the damn door Titus. I know you're both in here!"

I take back what I said. *William*. William could definitely ruin this moment.

Chapter Thirty-One

TITUS

"**W**hat the hell is your problem? Why didn't you tell me you'd found her." William rushes in as soon as I open the door, walking around the apartment like a mad man in search of his sister.

I stand there, waiting for him to stop moving before I speak. Once his eyes are on me, I let him know where he stands. "Brother, I understand your concern, but Ashley is mine to protect. She is safe now, washing up as we speak. Once she's feeling more like herself, she'll come out and talk to you."

William storms toward me, shoving me in an attempted show of dominance. "She is *my* sister and it's *my* duty to protect her. The least you could've done after defiling her was tell me where she was."

"I can assure you I was no virgin, William. There was definitely no defiling." Ashley's voice breaks into our staring match as she comes up behind me. "Please step the hell away from my fiancé."

Although there's a threat in her words, her tone is as sweet as honey. Waving her hand in William's awe-struck face, she begins to jump up and down. "That's right. You heard me. Titus asked me to marry him!"

I can't help but chuckle.

This woman is incredible. In two seconds flat, Ashley managed to diffuse a situation where her brother and I were at each other's throats.

Now, William looks like he doesn't know whether to congratulate us or punch me in the face.

"Um, congratulations?" William's brows scrunch together as he looks between Ashley and me. "I take it you two talked everything out?"

Ashley rolls her eyes while shoving at her brother. "Yes, no thanks to you. But it's okay. I forgive you. Especially since I know you'll forgive Titus and me for not telling you about us sooner."

This little minx bats her long lashes and it's as if her big brother is under her spell.

Note to self, beware of the lashes.

William shakes his head, trying to gather his thoughts after registering all the information he's received. "Okay. You two are engaged." William turns to me, glaring. "Don't think I'm forgiving you for not having asked for her hand first."

I scoff as Ashley snorts. "Like you would have given Titus your blessing!"

"That's beside the point. It's tradition."

"Since when have you known us to resemble anything close to traditional." It's my turn to snort.

William is definitely reaching.

"Anyway, we can celebrate the engagement later. Right now we have more pressing matters to handle. No thanks to you, I found out about Brad taking Ashley. So tell me, what did you do with the prick who drugged her up and tried to kill her? Where's the fucker now?"

"I'm surprised the team didn't tell you, since they told you I had Ashley and that she'd been seen by the doctor already."

William growls, "Those bastards didn't want to even tell me that much. They said something about it being disloyal."

I laugh, "At least our group of rent-a-cops are good for something."

William rolls his eyes, "Okay, well, where is he?"

Squeezing Ashley to me, I let my hand fall to the curve of her back before raising it and smacking her ass. "*Min skatt*, would you mind bringing me my phone?"

Her body stiffens, no doubt surprised by the sudden public display of affection. Well, she said she wanted me to declare her publicly. That's just what I'm doing.

Her eyes narrow but her lips tilt into a smirk. She very well knows what I'm doing, reading my actions like a book. "Yes," She follows that with a silent mouthing of 'Daddy' and my knees practically buckle in place.

Oh, she's definitely getting a spanking later.

As soon as she's out of ear shot, I fill William in. "I had the men take him to the warehouse. He's being picked up by the Renzetti Famiglia and they're putting him in a holding cell for me."

William raises a brow, "What exactly are you planning on doing with him?"

"He's my peace offering to you. To the team." I run my hand through my hair, unsure if this gift will be enough, but it's a start. "Since I didn't tell you about my feelings for Ashley, or how we've been together, I figured maybe this could soften the blow. You guys could pick the punishment for the prick who drugged and kidnapped a WRATH princess."

William's lips curl into a sneer. "How very thoughtful of you."

"So, what'll it be? What fate will you lay down for Brad?"

"I'll have to talk it over with the other men, but I have a feeling that the master of torture would be our pick." William shakes his head, probably wishing that this weren't the case.

"Who's the master of torture?" Ashley hands me my phone as she looks between her brother and me.

Taking her face in my hands, I tell her the truth. "I am, little treasure."

Her lips turn up, giving me a devilish smile. "That would make total sense."

William groans behind her, "Ugh. Enough with the PDA you two. A man could only take so much."

Taking Ashley's lips with mine, I whisper into her mouth. "Seems like that makes you the mistress of torture."

"You have no idea. Just you wait until I have you picking out centerpieces for our wedding."

I throw my head back and laugh a full bellied laugh, "Oh, *min skatt*. You're worth all of that torture and more."

Pressing a kiss to her lips, I let myself sink.

Deep into her.

Deep into love.

Deep into grace.

EXCERPT

Acts of Redemption

PROLOGUE

"**Y**ou worthless cunt."

A shove to my chest has my head flying backward, hitting the hardwood floor and releasing a loud echo into the conveniently empty room.

It's always empty. That's the way he likes it. No one to hear me cry. No one to see my tears.

"You should be kissing my feet, thanking me for everything I've given you." He crouches down onto the floor, breathing the words onto my neck as he pulls my head back, forcing me to look him in the eyes. "Remember, Charlotte... you are nothing without me."

His spittle lands on my face, but I don't flinch. Any movement on my part would only bring on more pain. *More torture.*

He finally releases my hair and begins to pace back and forth.

Motionless, like a broken rag doll, I remain on the ground— not wanting to draw any more attention to myself. He's silent for what feels like an eternity, and I pray it's a sign that he's ready to move on for the night.

Prayer. A fucking novelty, really.

I squeeze my eyes shut and give it one last shot.

God, if you're out there, please make this torture stop. Please end my pain.

A tear rolls down my cheek. The cold salty liquid stings as it reaches my split lip, reminding me I'm still here. Still living this hellish nightmare.

His steel-tipped cowboy boot connects with a punishing blow to my ribs, making me instinctively roll into the fetal position and shut my eyes.

"Ah, ah, ahh. Keep those pretty little eyes of yours open. I'm not done with you yet." His strong hands uncurl me from my position before reaching up for my nape, forcing me once again to face him.

Looking up at him, I see nothing but hatred and rage in his eyes, causing something in me to finally snap.

"*Why?* Why the fuck did you marry me if you hate me so much? If you won't believe me and just think the worst of me... then why?" my voice cracks—just like my soul, which is shattered beyond repair.

"Oh, Charlotte. Don't you see? You're my little doll. My play thing." He *tsks* as he shakes his head. "Every man of importance needs a trophy by his side."

This sick fuck. He never loved me. This is all a game to him. It's all a show.

I'm not a person, just a possession.

"Ah, that look in your face tells me you finally understand. Good. Maybe now you'll stay in line." He walks toward the door, but turns around before leaving me to clean up his mess. "You'll be getting new security detail, and no more whoring around with the staff. Those legs only open up for me."

And with those parting words, he's gone—leaving me a crumpled mess on the floor.

I roll on to my back and stare at the ceiling with its intricate design and gold leaf gilding. I wonder how many tragedies it's seen. I bet mine is nothing new, just one of many.

A tale of woe as old as time.

We are at a gala amongst the Dallas elite, yet no one will bat a lash when I re-enter the room with a split lip and a slight limp in my gait.

Don't ask, don't tell. That's their *modus operandi.* Lord knows there's nothing more uncouth than showing genuine emotion or concern.

I live in a world of fraud. Everyone and everything is fake. Plastic. Superficial.

Closing my eyes, I pick myself up, vowing to never let myself fall apart. Never let myself conform to their ways.

I fluff my unconventionally long black hair—a silent fuck you to the sea of blond that surrounds me—and straighten my dress.

Giving myself a mental pep-talk before I re-enter the world of dolls, I put on a smile.

Charlotte Annabelle Montgomery, this does not define you. You are worthy, you are special, and you will survive this.

Fuck anyone who stands in your way.

CHAPTER ONE

Charlotte

Coffee. The only delectable thing I'm looking forward to this morning.

Its rich aroma pulls me from the depths of my room and into

the kitchen where the beautiful Sandra is whipping up breakfast. She's been a godsend. The only person I can count on aside from myself in this godforsaken world of falsity.

And though I would trust Sandra with most things, there are still parts of my life I'd like to keep to myself.

Secrets are demons not to be shared. They lurk in the shadows, waiting to detonate and obliterate everyone and everything in their wake.

I've made that mistake before and paid dearly for it. *Never again.*

"Morning, Mrs. Rutherford. Would you like your egg white omelette now?" Sandra smiles at me while holding out a glorious cup of caffeine. Her rosy cheeks and beautiful silver hair make her the perfect Mrs. Claus doppelgänger, adding to her already likable personality.

"No thank you, Sandra. And please, just call me Charlotte."

Sandra's previously joyous face puckers as she looks at our surroundings before shaking her head repeatedly. "Oh, no. Mr. Rutherford has given me specific instructions. I'm never to address you so casually."

She spins around and busies herself with the already impeccably clean kitchen.

Spinning on my heels, I blow out a breath as I make my way back to my room. Figures the warden of my life would prevent anyone from getting close to me. Even my dear Sandra is off limits.

I'm about to close the door behind me when my husband's secretary buzzes through the intercom. "Mrs. Rutherford? Your new detail is here. The senator wanted you to meet with them immediately upon their arrival."

I press my forehead against the door and groan.

"What was that, Mrs. Rutherford?"

"Nothing. I'll be there in a minute. Thank you, Michaela."

I silence any further questioning by pushing the white button on the panel by the door. For a few brief moments, I'd forgotten about last night's ordeal. Ridiculous because my ribs still bear the imprint of Preston's boots.

Placing my mug on the nightstand, I stare toward my walk-in closet, contemplating throwing on a pair of sweats instead of the conservative black dress I know Preston would approve of.

Snickering, I pull on the matching grey sweater and pant set. I fancy it up by scrunching up the sleeves, throwing on my five inch Manolo Blahnik, and popping on a bright pink gloss to my lips, still bruised from the night before.

Content with my fashion choices for the day, I exit the room with my head held high. Let the bastard make a scene in front of people. Joke will be on him.

A new detail means that whoever is assigned to me will watch me like a hawk for the first couple of months until they let their guard down. This doesn't bode well for Preston and his alter-ego.

As I turn the corner, I see Sandra stealing glances into the parlor. *Interesting.* She's not usually one to butt her head into business other than hers.

The corner of my mouth lifts into a smirk, my right eyebrow cocking involuntarily. "What's so entertaining?" I whisper as I reach Sandra's side.

She jolts up, no doubt startled. "Mm—Mrs. Rutherford. Your new detail is here." Her face is pale, no longer holding any semblance of the rosiness I saw just moments ago.

My brows come together and my smile sours. Turning toward the sitting area, I see what's caused Sandra's concern.

Holy shit.

The men in the other room are drop dead gorgeous. Like something straight out of a GQ magazine. Wearing tailored suits that fit their body perfectly, there is no doubt that nothing but taught and tantalizing muscle lies underneath.

My eyes travel back and forth between the two men before me, and I'm about to push my mouth shut when I hear someone clearing their throat to my right.

Lord, help me. How did I miss him?!

If I thought the other two were GQ models, this one was sent straight from heaven. A deity walking this earth.

My eyes narrow as I study his face further. He looks familiar. But surely... *No. No. This cannot be happening.*

Like a freight train slamming into an unsuspecting vehicle, the memories assault me one by one.

His thick black hair, chiseled jaw, and piercing hazel eyes as rich as the tambour of his voice are enough to haunt my dreams for eternity.

Closing my eyes, I take a centering breath before entering the room. If I'm to survive the next six months I need to present the mother of all facades.

"Good morning, gentlemen. I'm Charlotte Rutherford." Stealing a quick glance toward tall, dark and handsome, I check to see if he's recognized me. I intentionally omitted my maiden name, and it's been decades since he's last seen me, so luck is on my side... at least I hope it is.

"Good morning, ma'am." The deity approaches me, not a hint of recognition in his beautiful eyes. "Name is Aiden Moretti. I'll be the lead assigned to you, however, Titus here will cover for me when I'm not on duty." He points toward one of the other men in the room who must be Titus.

Shifting my gaze back toward Aiden, I have to ask, "Has my husband met with you and your team, personally?"

"No, ma'am. We met with Michaela." After a beat, Aiden arches a brow. "Is there a problem?"

"Am I to believe Michaela gave you an itinerary and breakdown of my daily schedules, routines, and social engagements?" Completely ignoring his question, I power on. There's no way in hell I'm going to give him even an inkling of trouble in paradise. The last thing I need is for him to report back that I'm in some sort of trouble.

"Yes, ma'am." His tone is flat, lacking any emotion. But his eyes—those eyes—they tell me the truth. He hasn't missed the fact that I haven't answered his question and his eyes are trained on my bruised lip.

"Great, so you're aware of my meeting with the mayor's wife this afternoon. I have a couple of stops before I meet her for lunch. I'd like to leave in about thirty minutes."

"That won't be a problem, Mrs. Rutherford." His hazel eyes narrow, but no further comment follows.

Giving him a nod, I turn on my heels and head back to my room, needing to pick up my bag and the donations I'd compiled the last couple of weeks.

I'm about to reach my door when I hear heavy steps behind me. Whirling around, I almost run straight into a brick of chest. Slowly lifting my gaze upward, I'm met with the richest hazel eyes I've ever seen. Like deep pools of cashmere, I want to dive right in and envelop myself in their warmth.

"Ma'am, is everything okay?" His deep voice cuts into my thoughts and breaks me out of my trance.

"Yes, I'm not sure why you're following me. There's no need to follow me inside of the home." My brows furrow and my forehead crinkles. "This level of surveillance is unnecessary here."

"Mr. Rutherford begs to differ." That's it. That's all he gives me.

Well, shit. This is next-level smothering. Not only does Preston dictate who I can and cannot talk to, but he's now having me followed in my own home? If I felt like a prisoner before, now I'm definitely at Rikers.

Closing my eyes, I take in a deep breath. *Abort. Abort. Abort.* Huge mistake. Now all I'll be able to think of is the smell of Aiden's delicious scent of bergamot and cedarwood.

The scent takes me back to my childhood, where I was always the third wheel. Mother would never let Clarabelle go on dates alone, and it was little ol' me that got to witness her making out with the man of my dreams. Over and over again.

A hand to my shoulder startles me into opening my eyes. Once again, I'm looking into those beautiful pools of hazel, but now they're riddled with concern.

"You okay?" Two words. Oh, if he only knew.

"Yes." I sigh before smiling and shaking my head. "Well then, if that's what Mr. Rutherford wants, then that is what Mr. Rutherford gets." With a demure huff, I turn and enter my room to retrieve my bag and the tube of gloss I'd left on the vanity.

Looking in the mirror one last time, I see that Aiden is standing inside my room. Our eyes meet and I swear it's as if he's looking into my soul. The man can see me. Me and the skeletons I've shoved in my closet.

I clear my throat, needing to break the tension that's suddenly filled the air. "Right, well. We should get going."

I'm about to step past Aiden when his strong callused hand reaches out and grabs my arm, sending a current of electricity shooting straight through to my core. "Charlotte, is there anything I should know about?"

My eyes begin to tingle, the warning I need to snap me out of this weakened state. I will not cry in front of this man, nor will I let on about what dirty secrets I hold.

"Nothing you haven't been briefed on. Now if you'll please let me go, we have places to be, people to see, and things to do. If you'd like to help, you can carry those boxes out to the car. It will be our first stop."

Donning a sincere smile, I pray he lets it go. The last thing I need is for Preston to catch a whiff of my history with Aiden.

We'd have much bigger problems than his getting fired, and that's not a risk I'm willing to take.

Thank you for taking a chance on Acts of Salvation. If you loved it, please consider leaving a review.

It helps me tremendously!

MEN OF WRATH SERIES (forbidden love):

ACTS OF ATONEMENT
age-gap/nanny/single dad

ACTS OF SALVATION
age-gap/best friend's uncle

ACTS OF REDEMPTION
Brother's best friend

ACTS OF MERCY
age-gap/stepbrother

MAFIA ROMANCE:

OMERTA: A VERY MAFIOSO CHRISTMAS
Mozzafiato, prequel to MAGARI

MAGARI
Capo dei Capi falls for an outsider

FIND ME HERE:

Stay Connected

Let's stay connected. I'd love to hear what you thought of the book, what's on your TBR list, or simply how your day is going.

www.EleanorAldrick.com

Instagram
@EleanorAldrick

Goodreads
www.Goodreads.com/EleanorAldrick

Twitter
www.Twitter.com/EleanorAldrick

Facebook
www.Facebook.com/EleanorAldrick

Be sure to sign up for my <u>newsletter</u> where I share exclusive content. You won't want to miss out!

MVP ON REPEAT

Acknowledgements

I find it so surreal to be writing my fourth 'thank you' note to all of those who have stood by me on this crazy ass journey of becoming an author.

As this series nears its end, I'd like to thank my husband, who has gone above and beyond with his emotional support of my late-in-life career choice. I thank God every day for giving me a man who never belittles my passions or seeks to destroy my dreams. Instead, he encourages me and helps propel me forward when I just don't have the energy to continue. I love you, babe. You are, and always will be, the real MVP.

Second shoutout goes to the one and only, author V. Domino. Many friends have come and gone, but you have stood the test of time. Proving yourself to be a woman of amazing character, I'm proud to call you my honorary sister. On my darkest of days, when I've been riddled with self-doubt, you have pulled my head out of my ass and smacked me across the face, making sure to get me back in line. I love you, boo. You are the peanut butter to my jelly, the rock to my roll. We've got one more down, and many more to go.

Third shoutout goes to all the badass girlfriends, authors, and bookstagrammers who have kept the hype real and made this journey an incredible one. A big thank you to Ande, Stela, Nicole, Alicia Crofton, Sara, Priscilla, Marla, Tracy, J.M. Stoneback, Court, Kimberyle, M.D. Alexander and everyone on the street team. You all are a massive reason of who and where I am today. You inspire me to be better and make me push harder with everything that I do. You all are queens in your own right, and I am honored to call you a friend.

Last, but not least. You, the reader. Thank you for taking a chance on my book baby. It is my sincere hope that I was able to provide great entertainment and an enjoyable escape. Cheers to many more!

XOXO, Eleanor Aldrick

Made in the USA
Monee, IL
24 February 2023

28595532R00162